Kate Walker

A SICILIAN HUSBAND

ITALIAN
HUSBANDS

HARLEQUIN®

TORONTO • NEW YORK • LONDON
AMSTERDAM • PARIS • SYDNEY • HAMBURG
STOCKHOLM • ATHENS • TOKYO • MILAN • MADRID
PRAGUE • WARSAW • BUDAPEST • AUCKLAND

ISBN 0-373-12393-0

A SICILIAN HUSBAND

First North American Publication 2004.

Copyright © 2003 by Kate Walker.

Visit us at www.eHarlequin.com

Printed in U.S.A.

CHAPTER ONE

THE man at the other side of the bar was beautiful.

Beautiful.

Terrie could find no other word to describe him that fitted those devastating looks quite so well. And she had tried. Because *beautiful* didn't seem like quite the right word to use about someone so masculine, so totally male. And yet it was the only one that worked.

She'd tried *handsome* and it was too weak, too 'pretty' somehow. It didn't allow for the straight, firm slash of a nose, the sharply defined cheekbones. And *good-looking* was way too bland. This man was more than good-looking he was superb!

Attractive didn't even come near the truth, and, although *gorgeous* fitted with the lush warmth of his mouth, the stunning deep, deep brown of his eyes, the sleek olive skin that gave away the fact that he was most definitely not English, both *attractive* and *gorgeous* lacked the hard edge that this man wore like a suit of armour, the hint of danger that lurked in those deep-set eyes. And she suspected that that mouth, although apparently sensual, could soon harden to a dangerously cruel line.

His disturbing blend of supreme confidence, bordering on arrogance, and an aura of total ease in his surroundings and himself made him stand out in the crowded room as clearly as if a spotlight had been switched on, its beam centring on the glossy mane of jet-black hair.

No, *beautiful* was the only word that was right. He had a starkly masculine beauty that had caught and held her attention from the moment she had walked into the room. And now she couldn't drag her eyes away, even though she suspected that the intensity of her gaze must soon get through to him. Surely he would sense that someone was staring at him, feel it like a faint touch on his skin—and then he would look up.

And even as she thought it, the heavy-hooded lids that had been lowered suddenly lifted, and the burning golden-bronze eyes blazed into hers through lush black lashes.

And the look of cold disdain, the molten glare he turned on her, the obvious distance that he clearly wanted to put between them, was so clear, so sharply cutting that it made Terrie actually jump in her seat. Hastily she looked away again as quickly as possible. Heat screamed along the nerve paths of her body, searing a sense of burning embarrassment and humiliation at being caught staring like that. It was the behaviour of some lust-smitten ado-lescent confronted by the boy-band focus of her latest crush. She had never done anything quite so crass in her life before.

Stop it! she told herself in furious but silent reproof. Stop this nonsense right now!

The woman at the other side of the bar was staring straight at him, Giovanni Cardella realised. Staring straight at him with a mindless, dumbstruck expression on her face that made it look as if she had never seen a man before in her life. Sliding another glance in her direction through the concealment of thick, dark lashes, he frowned deeply, and dropped his eyes again to stare down into his glass.

Another woman.

Another woman who wasn't Lucia.

Another woman who was making it plain that she found

him attractive when that was the last thing on God's earth that he wanted.

He was no fool. He knew that he had the sort of looks, the colouring, the height, the build that drew female eyes his way. And that when their gaze rested on him, it lingered. As soon as it had become known that he was alone, they had been there. The female vultures had gathered, all seeking to 'comfort' the rich widower.

But he had no time, no inclination for other women. There had only ever been one woman in his life—Lucia. And Lucia had been all he had ever wanted.

And this woman was no Lucia. For one thing, she was a pale ash blonde with the sort of delicate complexion that came with the impossible weather on this rain-soaked island. And she was tall; even though she was sitting down he could tell that. Lucia had been petite; slight, dark and stunning. This woman, with her blue-grey eyes and fair hair, was like the opposite. The negative to Lucia's positive.

And she was still looking, damn her!

Today of all days, her bold stare felt like an invasion. It pushed into the privacy of his thoughts, intruded into his memories. And he hated that.

'Madre di Dio!'

Hot fury washed over him, driving him to lift his eyes again, when he would far rather have kept them fixed on the ground. His gaze swinging to her face in a rush, he turned on her a blazing glare that held all the force of the rejection of her unsubtle approach that burned in his soul.

'Oh, damn!' Terrie muttered under her breath, horrified by the response her unthinking reaction had caused. 'Damn, damn, damn!'

And the trouble was that even looking swiftly away and down at the table did nothing to ease the sensation of embarrassment and unease. She could still feel the scorch of his contempt searing over her skin, stripping her of a much-needed layer of protection.

'Well, it's time we got back.'

Beside her, Claire and Anna drained their glasses and made moves to get to their feet, picking up handbags, pushing back their chairs.

'You coming, Terrie?'

'What? No—I think I'll give this last session a miss.'

What was she doing? This was the perfect opportunity to sneak out of there, disappear before she made an even greater fool of herself. If she went now, then she and this man, the stranger she had been caught staring at, would probably—hopefully—never catch sight of each other again. If she could hide herself in the bustle and crowds of the conference she had come here to attend then hopefully he would forget about her and her *faux pas* would be overlooked as well.

But the truth was that she really didn't want to go. Even before she had come into the bar with her friends she had determined that the last session of the sales conference was more trouble than it was worth.

'Are you sure?'

Terrie nodded emphatically, shaking loose some of the blonde locks that she had forced into a hopefully disciplined chignon at the start of the day so that they fell in disordered tendrils around her oval face.

'Absolutely. I've been bored out of my skull from the start, and I really can't take any more. Before I came here, I was beginning to suspect that a career in selling baby clothes just wasn't for me—and now I'm absolutely positive that it's not. As soon as I get back to Netherton, I'm handing in my notice and looking for something else. So there's no point at all in my going back to hear the MD spouting about quotas and new lines.'

It sounded totally rational, clearly thought through. Nothing whatsoever to do with the fact that her sense of reality had just been severely rocked as a result of being confronted by the most devastating specimen of manhood she had ever seen. It had *nothing* to do with that, she told herself fiercely. Nothing at all.

'Well, if you've made up your mind.'

Claire still looked uncertain, but Anna was pulling at her sleeve, tugging her away towards the door through which the other conference delegates were already streaming, heading back to the ballroom.

'Definitely. I'm going to finish this drink and then go to my room and pack, ready for an early getaway tomorrow.'

'Then we'll see you at dinner?'

Terrie nodded abstractedly, her attention elsewhere. Until she had heard herself speak the words aloud, she hadn't really been aware that she planned to say them. But now that she had, she knew that she meant everything she'd said.

She *was* bored. If the truth was told, she hated her job. Hated the long hours and the travelling involved in it. Hated trying to persuade people to buy overpriced, second-rate items. She didn't know how she'd stuck it this long.

Well, from now on everything was going to change!

And for a start she wasn't going up to her room to pack after all. She was going to stay here and have another drink and relax. Recover from the endurance test that had been the sales conference.

And she wasn't even going to so much as *glance* in the direction of the wretched man on the other side of the room, she told herself as she got slowly to her feet. There was no way on earth that she wanted to risk another of those glares. She was still smarting from the scorching effect of the one she had already received.

Despite his determination not even to look in her direction again, Gio found that the woman's movement drew his attention once more. She uncoiled her slim body like a cat, he couldn't help reflecting, fascinated in spite of himself. Her movements were slow and sensual, the short stroll from her table to the bar making her slender hips sway underneath the deep red suit with its fitted jacket and narrow pencil skirt. The blonde hair was clearly fighting against the restraints of the too-severe knot she had twisted it up into, and feathery strands of it were blowing about her face, wafting onto her neck.

With a sigh of impatience that he caught even where he sat, she paused, reached up, pulled out a couple of strategically placed pins, and shook her head determinedly. The result caught Gio totally by surprise.

As the pale blonde swathe of hair came loose and tumbled down her back, flowing over her shoulders like a golden wave, he found himself suddenly a prey to an urgent, twisting pull of sensual demand low down in his body.

It had the force of a kick in his gut, hitting with the sort of intensity that he had thought that he would never experience again in his life.

'*Inferno!*' he swore under his breath, struggling to force his attention away and onto the narrow gold watch that encircled one wrist. Though even as he concentrated fiercely on its square face, he knew that every male instinct he possessed was still in a state of heightened awareness of the woman at the bar.

Where the devil *was* Chris Macdonald?

Drinks and a meal, and a chance to discuss how the day's events had gone in court, he had suggested, and the prospect had seemed like a lifesaver to Gio, who had been dreading spending the time on his own. Once he'd talked to Paolo on the phone and wished his little son sweet dreams, the evening had stretched ahead empty and dark, filled with bad memories. He had snatched at the opportunity to have company on this, the anniversary of the worst night ever in his life.

But Chris showed no sign at all of putting in an appearance. Their meeting had been arranged for six, and it was now half past.

The realisation had barely crossed his mind when his mobile phone rang sharply. As if summoned by his thoughts, there was Chris Macdonald's number on the screen.

Flicking the case open with an impatient hand, Gio lifted it to his mouth.

'*Sì?*'

A few seconds later he snapped the phone off again and tossed it down onto the table, glaring at it as if the inoffensive gadget were in fact Macdonald himself.

Chris was not coming. He had to stay at home, he had said. His young daughter was ill and they had just called the doctor.

'*Non c'e problema!*' he had assured him. 'Don't worry about it.'

But he had been lying through his teeth. There *was* a problem. The problem of the long, lonely night that lay ahead of him.

He should be used to long, lonely nights. He'd lived through enough of them since he had lost Lucia. Lying awake, staring blank-eyed into the darkness, in the big, empty bed that had suddenly seemed so cold and uncomfortable without the warmth of her softly curvaceous body beside him.

And if he managed to fall asleep then it was even worse. Because then he woke to a moment of forgetfulness, a brief, merciful spell of believing that it had never happened. That she was still there, with him. Until he reached out and felt the coldness of the empty space beside him, and the reality all came flooding back.

'*Dio—no!*' he muttered savagely, both hands clenching into fists as he tried to push away the black thoughts that flooded his mind.

Tonight he had thought that he would escape them. That with friendly company, a meal, and perhaps a glass or two too many of a fine wine, he might find some relief from the emptiness that was always there, like a dark, dangerous chasm in his mind, just waiting for him to fall into it. But Chris's phone call had just shattered that hope.

'And what can I get for you, Miss Hayden?'

'Dry white wine, please.'

Behind him, Gio heard the bartender's question, the soft, feminine tones of the reply, and knew without a moment's hesitation that it was the blonde who had spoken. The blonde who had been eyeing him up so blatantly.

'Your friends not with you tonight, then?' The bartender almost echoed Gio's own thoughts.

'No, they've gone into the final session of the conference. I'll be joining them later for dinner, I suppose.'

'You didn't fancy going with them?'

'No.'

He could almost hear the shudder in her voice.

'I've had more than enough of sales figures and targets. I've been bored stupid the past two days; I couldn't take any more. In fact, I've decided to chuck the job in.'

Bored, huh?

The word seemed to echo inside Gio's head. She was bored, and she had been eyeing him—and she had deliberately stayed behind when her friends had left.

Coincidence or invitation?

The clamour in his body wasn't easing. If anything, the sound of her voice had made it worse. It was soft, musical, and faintly husky. The sort of voice that made him think of murmurs in the darkness of the night, the heat of a sensual bed, the whisper of her breath across his skin as she spoke.

And it had been so long. Too long for any red-blooded male.

'This conference has been no fun at all. I've decided I need some other way of making a living. So I think I'll just hang around here for a while and see what happens.'

The thread of laughter through the words was the last straw. It seemed to carry an electrical charge with it, sparking off hot little arrows of hunger that ran along every nerve, bringing them so stingingly awake that he had to bite his lip to keep back the groan of reaction.

So she wanted *fun*, did she? And he...he wanted anything, *anything* other than to be alone for another long, dark night. He wanted a warm, living, breathing, responding body in his bed after far, far too long.

He hadn't felt this interested, this alert, this *alive* in years. And he wasn't going to turn his back on the chance to let this feeling continue for as long as he could.

He was on his feet before he had actually finished the thought, turning and heading for the tall, slender figure at the bar.

Terrie rested her elbows on the polished wood, stared down into the cool, clear liquid in her glass and wondered just what she had done.

Burned her boats, the answer came back from the sensible, rational part of her mind. She had well and truly burned her boats, or her bridges, cut off her nose to spite her face... Insert whatever other clichéd sayings described her uncharacteristically rash and unthinking gesture.

She was probably in trouble with her job, for one. James Richmond, her immediate manager, would have noticed her absence from the MD's speech and she had no doubt that he would haul her into his office as a result. He was that sort of man. And people just did *not* skip what he considered to be vital parts of this conference— at least, not with impunity. The last time that had happened, the offending person had been shown the door pretty fast.

So even if she didn't resign herself, she was almost certainly unemployed. And, as a result, in financial difficulties, owing rent on her flat, and with no way to keep up payments on her car. OK, so her job had been a bore and a grind. But it had been a job. One that paid her way at least. And she had put it at risk on some foolish, impossible impulse that she couldn't even explain to herself.

That man. The thought rushed into her mind, driving everything else before it.

It had been the sight of the beautiful man at the other side of the bar that had somehow pushed her into this crazily impulsive mood. The sort of stupid, irrational mood in which she threw up a perfectly decent job and behaved in a way that meant she just didn't recognise herself.

For example—just *what* was she doing standing here, propping up this bar, when everyone else was completing the schedule of the conference before the final dinner and going home? What was she waiting for? Hoping for?

Did she really think—was she actually *hoping* that the

stunning and exotic-looking stranger was going to come up to her and change her life?

Fat chance!

Terrie actually snorted cynically at the idiotic path of her own thoughts. She really couldn't believe *that!*

Picking up her glass, she twisted on her heel, turning so that she was half facing the rest of the bar, but at an angle so that if the intriguing stranger was looking again she wouldn't risk being seen by him. Just one experience of that furiously cold-eyed glare was bad enough. She didn't want to go through a repeat performance.

The wretched man had actually gone!

'Well, thanks a bunch!' Terrie muttered against the rim of her glass as she lifted it to sip at her wine. 'Thank you so very much!'

Foolishly, she felt as if he was responsible for the pickle she was in. She had made this crazy, impulsive gesture of throwing in her job in some non-typical response to his presence. Had stayed in the bar when she would have been far better to stick with her friends and go to the final session, however boring. Had even...

Admit it! she declared to herself. She had even hung around in the bar in the hope of meeting up with and discovering more about this man who had had such an impact on her.

And the so-and-so had got up and made his way out of the bar while her back was turned, without so much as a second look. He must have walked within inches of her and she hadn't even noticed!

So much for changing her life at a stroke!

Scowling as much at her own foolishness as at the absent stranger, Terrie lifted her drink in a bleak parody of a toast, inclining it in the direction of the stranger's now empty seat.

'To ships that pass in the night,' she muttered.

And froze as, from her right-hand side, another hand reached out, deliberately clinking the glass it held against hers in acknowledgement of the toast.

'Salute, signorina!' a deep, lyrically accented voice murmured in her ear.

CHAPTER TWO

'WHAT?'

The shaken exclamation was pushed from her lips as her nerveless fingers lost their grip on her glass. Slipping from her grasp, it tumbled downwards, spilling its contents on the way, and crashed onto the floor, splintering into a thousand tiny pieces.

'Oh, look what you've done now!'

Even as the words escaped her, she was acknowledging how irrational they were. It was her own disturbed feelings that had twisted her nerves so tight she was ready to jump like a startled cat at the slightest thing. And as for feeling that seeing him had somehow pushed her into making rash decisions about her life, well, that was just nonsense. She had been ready to make a move long before she had ever set eyes on him.

But acknowledging that fact and reacting accordingly were two totally different things. Especially when she was now up so close to him that she could see that his eyes were closer to bronze than ebony and that fascinating little gold flecks burned like slivers of flame at the heart of their irises.

'Perdone, signorina.'

The voice was even more devastating close up, too. Pure warm, liquid honey, with just the tiniest touch of gravel in its husky undertone.

'Forgive me...your skirt...'

A long tanned hand lifted in an autocratic summons to the bartender, and before Terrie even had time to realise just what he had in mind a clean, damp cloth had been provided without a word having to be spoken. The next moment she found herself looking at the top of the stranger's downbent head, staring fascinated at the sheen on the night-dark strands, as he set himself to wiping away the splashes of wine from her skirt.

And this was worse than ever. The stroke of the cloth over the lower part of her body, even with the linen of her skirt acting as a buffer, made her heart thud unevenly, her breath catch in her throat. And when he moved lower, wiping away a few glistening droplets that were clinging to the fine nylon of her stockings, she shifted uneasily, uncomfortably.

He was too close. Far, far too close. If she inhaled she could breathe in some shockingly sensual scent. The tang of bergamot and lemon, mixed with the other, more intensely personal aroma of his skin.

'No—it's all right... Please...'

Her skin was prickling with sensation, heat racing through her veins. And when the side of his hand brushed her leg, skin almost touching skin, she had to clamp her mouth tightly shut, teeth digging into her lower lip, against the moan of response that almost escaped her.

'It will dry!' she declared with more emphasis than was necessary. Anything to stop him, to distract him from these disturbingly intimate attentions. 'And it's only a cheap suit.'

'Then let me at least buy you another drink.'

Terrie was so relieved by the way he straightened up, tossing the cloth onto a nearby table, that she would have agreed to anything. She didn't spot the look or gesture with which he summoned the bartender, barely heard the swift commanding notes of his order. Yet somehow he had manoeuvred her into a seat at the far side of the room, settling her on the burgundy velvet chair before taking the one opposite her in the privacy of the booth. And the next moment a full glass was brought and placed carefully in front of her.

'It was dry white wine, wasn't it?'

'Oh—yes…'

Her response was even more distracted because as he lounged back in his seat and stretched out his long legs in front of him, crossed at the ankles, she discovered to her horror that her skirt had not been the only victim of the accident with the glass. The smart silver-grey trousers that were now in her view were liberally splashed with wine too—and his was only too clearly *not* a cheap suit. In fact, if the perfect fit, immaculate tailoring and fabulous material were anything to go by, it was an extremely expensive item of clothing.

'But there's no need… You don't have to go to any trouble.'

'It is no trouble,' he assured her, his voice low and as intent as the gleaming eyes that were fixed on her face. 'On the contrary, it's a pleasure.'

The words should have been reassuring, but to Terrie's total consternation they had precisely the opposite effect. She felt uncomfortably as if someone had scraped away a vital protective layer from her skin, leaving her nerves raw and uncomfortable, and that unnervingly direct stare made her shift uneasily on the velvet-covered chair.

Up close, he was just *too much*. Too beautiful, too big, too sexually disturbing, too *male*, for any female with the normal amount of hormones to be able to cope. And every single one of Terrie's feminine instincts was on buzzing red alert at simply being faced with him.

'I really think…'

'What are you afraid of?'

'I'm not *afraid*!'

Her tone of voice belied it, starting high-pitched and rising even further until it ended in an inelegant squawk at the end of the sentence.

'Then drink your wine.'

Softly spoken as it was, it was clearly a command, and one he intended to have obeyed at once and without question. Just for a second Terrie was tempted to argue. But the impulse to rebellion died as soon as she looked into his dark face and met the forceful blaze of those tawny eyes head-on.

'Thank you,' she managed, reaching for the glass.

But with the drink halfway to her lips she suddenly paused again.

'I wouldn't want you to think...I mean—I don't normally let...'

To her embarrassment, the faint lift of one black eyebrow mocked the struggle she was having to get her words out.

'I don't normally talk to strange men in bars.'

Was she truly as nervous as she sounded? Gio wondered. Or was it just an act? Surely the woman who had given him such a deliberate and unashamed appraisal couldn't now be feeling uncertain and ill at ease.

Wasn't it more likely that, having won his interest, she had now decided to change tactics, preferring to act as the prey rather than the hunter? Well, he would play along for the moment, though he wasn't in the mood for subtlety or games. And as they were both only after one thing, then quite frankly he didn't see the need for them.

'And I don't normally talk to women I don't know either,' he returned smoothly.

If he had had any doubts about the way he was going to handle this, then they had evaporated as soon as he had seated himself opposite her. This woman had class. The slim, elegant body, the fall of pale blonde hair, the porcelain-pale complexion, all had a touch of exoticism to a man used to being surrounded by women with a much darker natural colouring. The faint scent of her body mixed with a light, floral perfume to send a sensual message straight to his brain, making his body harden in hungry demand. But rushing things would be a mistake. The evening would be much more enjoyable if he took his time, enjoyed the journey as well as the final arrival at his destination.

And the final conquest would be all the sweeter as a result.

'So why don't we introduce ourselves and then neither of us will be complete strangers?'

One long, powerful hand was held out over the table, the fingers elegant and square-tipped.

'My name is Giovanni Cardella. But most of my friends call me Gio.'

He pronounced the name like a softened version of 'Joe', though in his beautiful accent it had nothing like the ordinary solidity of the English form.

'Terrie Hayden...'

Did she really have to touch that hand? She had reacted badly enough to the brief, faint brush of it against her leg. How much worse would she feel if she had to grasp those strong-boned fingers, feel the heat of that satin olive skin against her own?

But it seemed she had no choice. Taking a deep breath, she put her own hand into his, sharp white teeth digging into her lower lip as his strength closed around her. The sensation of grasping a live electrical wire sent a powerful, burning reaction zigzagging up her arm, making her head swim so that she missed Gio's murmured response.

'I'm sorry?'

'Terry?' he repeated, frowning faintly. 'But that is a man's name—no?'

'It's Terrie—with an i and an e, not a y.'

Carefully she eased her hand away from his, struggling to resist the impulse to cradle it against her, as if his touch had actually burned her skin.

'It's short for Teresa actually. But, like you, no one ever calls me by my proper name.'

'I would. Terrie is not right for you—but Teresa...'

He made it sound so very different, Terrie registered with a sense of shock. After so many years of being called *Tereesa*, then his lyrical pronunciation of *Terayza* had a lovely, musical sound that made her smile unconsciously.

'I will call you Teresa.'

He could call her anything he liked, if he would just continue to speak to her in that wonderful voice; if he would smile into her eyes in that enticing way. The effect of that smile was to make her feel as if she was bathed in the warm sun of some Mediterranean country, which was obviously where he had been born.

'What part of Italy are you from?' she asked impulsively.

'I am a Sicilian. My home is in Palermo.'

It fitted. Italy would have given him the smooth sophistication that he wore with the sleek ease of an elegant cat. And Sicily had added the dangerous, untamed streak that burned in the tawny eyes, the curl of his mouth. Knowing he came from Sicily was like opening the door to the family pet cat, only to find that in its place a dark, dangerous, predatory jaguar had prowled into the room.

'I'd love to visit Sicily! I've never been further abroad than a weekend trip to Bruges, and I'd really like to travel more.'

'Well, perhaps now that you've decided to ''chuck the job in'' you'll get the chance to do just that.'

At first Terrie thought that it was just the way that the slang phrase sounded strange on his tongue that made her pause, considering it thoughtfully. But next moment came the stunning realisation that he was quoting her own words directly, making her head whirl in shock.

'Chuck the—you heard that! You were listening!'

'You weren't exactly quiet. I wasn't aware that what you were saying was a state secret. If you hadn't wanted anyone else to hear then you should have kept your voice lower.'

Was she really trying to pretend that she hadn't meant him to 'overhear'? After that openly interested look, the way that she had announced that she was bored and looking for some fun was a deliberate come-on if ever he'd heard one. It was too late for her to back down now.

And, if the truth was told, he would be disappointed if she did. He had no time for games, for the two steps forward, one step back dance of seduction. For the flirtatious pretence of needing to be wooed in order to be won. He knew what he wanted out of this—and, he was sure, so did she. So why were they playing around?

'Have dinner with me.'

'What?'

The question came so sharply, so unexpectedly that it caught Terrie totally off guard. It also caught her midswallow of another sip of wine and she had to close her mouth hurriedly and gulp it down hard so as not to choke.

'What did you say?' she asked, lavender eyes opening wide in apparent shock.

Was this not what she wanted, then? Of course it was, so why did she look so startled, as if the invitation was a total surprise? Or was it that he had acted too fast, cut through some of the expected moves, the polite chat, the 'getting to know you' that she had been anticipating?

Hadn't she expected him to be quite so forthright?

Well, he wasn't in the mood for observing convention, even if waiting increased the pleasure for her.

'Have dinner with me. Oh, come on, *mia bella*! Don't look so shocked! It's not as if I've asked you to come to bed with me right here and now. It's only dinner.'

Only dinner! Terrie's head was spinning with the suddenness and the shock of it all. It was only—what?—less than half an hour since she had first spotted this man on the opposite side of the room. No more than twenty minutes since he had caught her eye and given her the most furiously off-putting glare it had ever been her misfortune to encounter. Then he had sneaked up on her, frightened her into dropping her glass, and now...

'You want me to have dinner with you?'

'And is that so hard to understand?'

The beautiful voice had developed a hard edge that reminded her unnervingly of the glare he had turned on her earlier.

'I know English is not my first language, but I would have thought...'

'Your English is perfect and you damn well know it! But after the look you gave me a while ago—when you were sitting over there...' Terrie waved a hand in the direction of the Sicilian's previous seat. 'I would have thought that you couldn't wait to see the back of me.'

'Ah, that...'

Gio had the grace to look a little shamefaced. The sensual shape of his mouth twisted slightly as he swirled the last drops of his wine round and round in the bottom of his glass.

'That wasn't meant for you,' he murmured, his attention apparently fixed on the rich red liquid. 'I was angry with someone else—someone I had expected to meet.'

'Another woman?'

Of course. It figured. He had been stood up and now he wanted to fill the unexpectedly empty hours with someone else.

'Well, you certainly know how to make a girl feel second best.'

'*Come?*'

Those heavy lids flew up, stunning eyes fixing on her face, his confusion apparently genuine.

'No—you have it totally wrong. The man I was supposed to meet was someone I work with—it was a business meeting. He rang a short time ago to say that he couldn't make it.'

'So you're all on your own?'

She tried to make it sound grudging, as if she was not fully mollified, but only succeeded in coming across as making a hasty reassessment and coming close to conceding.

'All on my own—a stranger lost in London... You don't believe me?'

Her expression had given her away.

'You're no more lost than I am! Less, in fact. You look more at home here than I do. In fact I'd be willing to bet that you know your way around London as well as you do Palermo.'

'I'll concede you that.'

The admission was accompanied by another of those smiles that had the force of a thousand-watt electrical charge, the effect of it sizzling straight through every single nerve in her body and making her toes curl in instant reaction inside her elegant court shoes.

'But I *am* still on my own. And I'm hungry. And I

would prefer to have company while I eat rather than spend the rest of the evening alone. I have a table booked for two. It would seem a waste not to use it, when you are looking for company too.'

Something about that 'looking for company' snagged on a raw edge in Terrie's mind, making her hesitate sharply. But even as she was rethinking hastily he leaned forward and looked straight into her eyes, fixing her with the hypnotic force of his deep, dark gaze.

'*Per piacere,*' he said softly, huskily. 'Please have dinner with me.'

She *should* say that she was having dinner with her friends—with the rest of the conference. She was *going* to say exactly that. She actually opened her mouth to form the words, only to hear herself say exactly the opposite.

'Yes,' she managed a touch breathlessly. 'Thank you.'

If he had put one foot wrong in his reaction... If he had so much as looked in the least bit self-satisfied or triumphant, then she would have retracted immediately. She would have rushed to her feet, told him that no, she'd changed her mind, she was already booked for this evening. She would have rejoined Claire and Anna and eaten the buffet meal that came as part of the conference package. And, although she would have probably always regretted not accepting his invitation, she would have told herself that it was safer this way—that she wasn't putting herself at any sort of risk.

But Giovanni Cardella did nothing of the sort.

Instead he simply reached out one long, elegant hand. The bronzed fingers touched hers where they lay on the polished wood table-top, rested lightly, warmly, briefly— just for a moment—and then lifted and moved to pick up his glass once again.

'Thank you,' he said, lifting it to his lips and draining

the last of his wine. 'Shall we go through to the restaurant?'

And as she nodded silently Terrie admitted to herself that it had been the brevity of that touch that had been her undoing. Delicate and swift, it had been like the feel of a butterfly alighting and then flying away again. And it had left her feeling lost and unsatisfied. It had just been enough to awaken those electric feelings that had fizzed over her skin. Awaken them and then leave them—and she wanted more. Much, much more.

She didn't know whether it was those feelings, or simply coincidence, but as she got up from her chair to follow him she caught her foot on something and stumbled awkwardly.

At once Gio was at her side, hands coming out to support her, powerful arms taking her full weight with only the faintest tensing of muscle to reveal any effort. And as he held her close, her cloud-coloured eyes flew to his and locked with ebony darkness.

'Careful!' The single word shivered over her skin.

Would he kiss her now? Terrie wondered, the question flaring so swiftly in her mind, burning so fiercely that she felt sure that Gio must see it in her eyes and recognise her need in an instant. And it was that need that stunned her, shaking her rigid because she had never felt anything like it before in her life.

Oh, she had been attracted to men, obviously, in her past. She had even come close to wondering if she was in love. But nothing had lasted. Nothing had taken root and settled and flowered into something greater, something stronger, something...

Something *permanent*?

Just the thought shocked her rigid.

No, she had to be kidding. Had to be fooling herself.

Jumping in feet first where someone wiser and more thoughtful would hold well back. Feelings like that didn't just hit home and set in the space of a couple of seconds. They took time to grow, to develop and become a vital part of you. They came with knowledge and understanding and she knew little enough about this Giovanni Cardella—and understood less.

'Th-thank you.'

She didn't know if it was the stumble or the realisation of what she was feeling that put the tremor into her voice. She only knew that she needed to touch him—really touch him! Feel that smooth olive skin without the barrier of his jacket or hers in between.

And so she lifted her hand, raising it to his face. And let her fingers rest against his cheek, lying along the hard line of his jaw, supremely sensitive to the warmth of his flesh, the power of bone, the faint roughness where the hairs of his beard lay just below the surface of his skin.

'Thank you,' she said again, amazed that this time her voice sounded stronger when inside her stomach the nerves were twisting themselves into tight, painful knots, squeezing harder and harder with each breath she took.

'*Di niente.* No problem.'

His hand touched hers again, pressing it softly against his cheek. Then his fingers closed around hers, lifting them, turning them so that he was looking straight down on to the delicate tips, the oval-shaped, shell-pink painted nails.

'No problem,' he murmured again, but with a very different intonation this time. One that Terrie struggled to interpret.

But, even as she was reaching mentally for the indecipherable note in his voice, he moved again, and this time he blew her thought process right out of focus. He lifted the hand he held; lowered his head towards it. And when his mouth and her fingers met he pressed a long, lingering kiss first on their tips and then, slowly and sensually, all the way to the back of her hand.

'Gio…'

His name was just a sigh from her lips, faint as a breath, and she was stunned and bewildered to find that sudden tears stung her eyes. Tears of confusion and delight. Of almost fearful sensitivity to each and every movement that this man made.

Did he know what he was doing to her? Did he realise that, when she was used to the fumbling, clumsy, grabbing advances of men closer to her own twenty-four years, his gentleness, his gallantry—his *courtship*—were infinitely more seductive than any more passionate approach?

A moment before, she had longed for his kiss. The image of him taking her mouth in passion had flared in her mind like the blaze of lightning. But he had kissed her hand, and the delicacy of the gesture, the gentleness of his touch, had had so much more power over her feelings than any more overt approach.

'I'd love to have dinner with you,' she managed, needing to say something to show him a touch of what she was feeling, and yet afraid to let him in fully. To reveal just how deeply he had affected her.

His smile was swift, flashing on and off with the speed of a neon sign.

'I thought we'd already agreed on that.'

This was going exactly the way he wanted it, Gio reflected as he took her arm to lead her out of the bar and towards the ornate glass doors into the restaurant. At least now Terrie—*Terrie!* What sort of a name was that for a woman? Now that Terrie had stopped pretending that she needed to be persuaded to spend time with him, they both understood what the evening was all about.

She had wanted him to kiss her a moment ago. It had shown in her face. But a kiss was not what he had in mind. At least not a kiss on the mouth. The only woman he had kissed on the lips since Lucia had been Megan. Gio let a brief, fleeting smile cross his lips at the thought of his new and hugely pregnant sister-in-law. She had brought some much-needed warmth into his half-brother's life and, he admitted, into his own. Megan he would kiss and hug willingly. And his mother. No one else.

And certainly not this woman. Not some passing stranger he had picked up in a bar purely at the prompting of his most basic masculine urgings. A one-night stand was all it was. All it could ever be. And Teresa understood that. For a moment there he had had his doubts, but the way she had accepted his invitation to dinner, the carefully staged stumble so that he would be forced to take her in his arms, had reassured him of the facts. She knew exactly what was going on; how to play this game.

It should be plain sailing from now on. A meal. Some social chat. A touch of flattery, some light flirtation across a candlelit table. A shared bottle of wine—a nightcap…

And they would share that nightcap in her room. Her room, not his. Taking her to his room implied more than he meant her to take away from this encounter. And, after the nightcap, they would share a bed.

For tonight. And for tonight only.

And tomorrow he would go on his way—alone.

CHAPTER THREE

'SO WHAT are you doing in England? You don't look like a tourist and you said you'd planned on meeting someone from work. A business meeting?'

Gio nodded slowly, dark eyes shadowed in the candle-light.

'I'm a lawyer—and we were to discuss how the case went in court today. A post-mortem if you like.'

'And how did the case go?'

'We won.' It was said with total calm; no hint of any false modesty.

Of course he'd won. Gio didn't look as if he had ever known failure or defeat in his life.

A faint touch of wary apprehension slid coldly down her spine just at the thought. She wouldn't like to come up against Giovanni Cardella in court. He would have to be counsel for the prosecution, and she just knew that his approach would be deadly, his questions swift and lethal as a cobra's strike. In fact she wouldn't want to come up against Gio in any situation. He would be a formidable opponent, whatever the circumstances.

'Was it an—an important case?'

She stumbled over the question because her treacherous mind chose just that moment to throw at her the image of another, totally different way she could possibly be *against* Gio. For a few, feverish seconds, her imagination ran riot at the thought of how it might feel to be held close to that lean, hard body, crushed against the wall of his chest in the grip of those powerful arms that the sleek tailoring of his jacket did nothing to disguise.

'Important enough. International fraud—a man who's been making millions… What are you smiling at?'

'Nothing—I mean—I didn't know I was…'

The pictures her wayward thoughts had been conjuring up of the way the devastating man opposite her might look with the sophisticated elegance of the jacket and shirt stripped away vanished in a second as the bubble of her fantasy was popped by his probing question. For a moment her hands wavered uncertainly in front of her face while she struggled with the temptation to cover her burning cheeks and hide behind them, away from his searching gaze. But then she forced them down again, reaching instead for her wine glass and taking a much-needed restorative sip.

'If you must know I was feeling like Cinderella at the ball. I mean—all this…'

The hand that held her glass waved rather wildly as she used it to indicate her luxurious surroundings, the heavy linen tablecloths, the silverware and crystal glasses, the immaculately uniformed waiters, their footsteps hushed on the thick, rich pile of the red and gold carpet.

'It's hardly how I was expecting to spend my evening.'

A sudden memory slid into her mind. The image of Claire and Anna, just emerging from the doors of the conference room, their mouths agape and a look of total consternation and disbelief on their faces as they had seen her crossing the foyer with Gio at her side. By rights she should be with them now, sharing the cold buffet, thinking about packing, about leaving tomorrow morning.

She could only pray that Gio hadn't seen them too. That he hadn't caught the way they'd stopped dead, giggled, nudged each other, and then, most embarrassingly of all, given her a blatant 'thumbs up' sign of approval.

'I was thinking that if I pinched myself I might suddenly wake up and find it was all a dream.'

'And that I had turned into a pumpkin, hmm? Isn't that how the story goes?'

'Oh, no. Not at all! Prince Charming wasn't transformed into anything. He stayed a prince all the way through.'

'And is that how you see me?' His tone was casual enough but there was an unexpected light in his eyes, one that made every tiny hair on the back of her neck suddenly lift in nervous apprehension. 'Am I truly Prince Charming?'

Was he? Was he really the person he seemed? The delightful, easy-going dinner companion, the man who was politeness personified. Who had told her to order whatever she wanted from the menu, who made sure that her every need was attended to—her meal served, her glass filled, her plate cleared, even before she had realised that she wanted anything herself. Was this the real Giovanni Cardella or was there another side to him? What about the man who appeared in court?

'You certainly can be charming when you choose,' she said carefully.

'Choose?'

'Well—I get the feeling that you've deliberately set out to be this way. That you mean to be nice to me. That you—'

'And why would I not?' Gio cut in with a touch of sharpness. 'You are a woman—and a beautiful one at that. Wouldn't any man want to treat you like this? Wouldn't any sane male want to "charm" you, to please you? To see you smile?'

'I have to admit that it's not exactly what I'm used to,' Terrie murmured, totally thrown off balance by that softly emphasised 'beautiful'. 'The men that I've dated haven't had your…flair—your skill—at this. Or the money to bring me here, for that matter.'

'And the money is important?'

Gio recognised his mistake as soon as the words were out. Those soft grey eyes flew to his face, narrowing sharply as she caught the note of cynicism in his voice. So the lady didn't want the truth being stated too openly? Well, he could go along with that. Part of his attraction for her might be that he obviously had the wealth to give her a good time, but she clearly preferred to pretend that it went deeper than that.

'I'm not—' Terrie began indignantly.

'You're the one who described yourself as Cinderella at the ball,' Gio pointed out with calm reasonableness. 'I got the impression that you weren't used to being in a place like this. Was I wrong?'

'Well—no…' Terrie was forced to admit. 'I don't normally end up in posh restaurants—or hotels for that matter. It's only because I was at this conference and the company's paying that I'm here at all.'

'The company that you have now decided you no longer want to work for?'

'The same.' Terrie nodded, her expression rueful. 'So I expect that this will be my one and only taste of such luxury for a long, long time. I can't expect fairy godfathers to come along every day of the week, can I?'

She looked deep into his eyes as she spoke, her lavender-coloured gaze wide and intent above the soft, full mouth. Watching her, Gio felt desire give him such a hard, demanding kick that he shifted uncomfortably in his chair.

'A moment ago I was Prince Charming, now you've cast me in the role of Fairy Godfather.'

Or she'd like to put him in that role. Well, if a long-term sugar daddy was what she was after then she was doomed to disappointment.

'Perhaps you're both?'

Though of course there was no way that the 'Fairy' part of the description fitted, Terrie reflected, her whole body tingling in sensual awareness of the strength and power of the hard masculine body seated opposite her. One lean brown hand rested on the starched tablecloth, the tanned skin standing out sharply against the crisp white damask, and, having dropped her gaze to it for a moment, she suddenly found herself unable to drag her eyes or her thoughts away again.

What would it feel like to have those long, strong fingers caress her skin? How would his touch move over her sensitive flesh? Would it be soft and tantalising or hard and demanding? Every female instinct told her that he was a man who would know how to love a woman. How to arouse her, to stir her senses until she was barely conscious with longing, to set her whole body quivering...

Oh, lord, what *was* she doing? Just to think like this was turning her on, making heated passion uncoil in yearning demand in the pit of her stomach. Clumsily she reached for her glass, swallowing down some of the wine in an attempt to ease the sudden dryness of her throat.

'Of course, I suppose to you this is quite common-place,' she blurted out, desperate to move the conversation along and so distract herself from her wanton thoughts. 'You must always be in places like this.'

'My legal work takes me all over the world.'

'That must be exciting—working in so many different countries.'

'Not really.'

Gio shrugged off her comment.

'When you've seen one hotel room, you've seen them all. And usually I'm working so hard that I don't get to see anything of the places where I'm staying.'

And that was how he liked it. The truth was that he didn't *need* to work; not financially at least. Thanks to the huge corporation owned by their joint families, both he and his half-brother Cesare were independently wealthy enough never to have to work again if they didn't feel like it.

But working filled the long, empty hours of the day. It tired him so that at least he had some hope of sleeping at night and it stopped him from thinking—from remembering.

'That's a terrible pity! Such a waste. I'd love to see all those—'

'I'm there to work,' Gio interrupted crushingly. 'And at the end of a long day in court I'm hardly in the mood for sightseeing.'

Perhaps now she'd get the message that he wasn't prepared to listen to her unsubtle hints.

Leaning back in his chair, he too reached for his wine glass and sipped at his drink slowly, all the while watching the woman before him. Did he care that she was so obviously attracted by his wealth? he asked himself. And that she was trying to insinuate that maybe they could spend some time together?

No. Quite frankly, he didn't give a damn. He was in the mood for some female company tonight—and for tonight only. And because of that he couldn't care less what she found attractive about him. Only that she did find him attractive. Because with those huge, soft eyes, the tumble of pale hair, the moist, inviting mouth, she was the sexiest thing he'd seen in a long time.

Did she know the way the candlelight caught on her hair, raising sparks of brilliant gold in the ash-blonde strands? Was she aware of the way that it gave her skin a softly luminous sheen, like the glow on a string of the finest freshwater pearls? And had she sensed that when she leaned forward to talk to him the low V-neck of the white cotton top she wore gaped slightly, giving him a tantalisingly erotic glimpse of the shadowed, perfumed valley of her cleavage?

Of course she had! In fact, he suspected her of making that movement quite deliberately, knowing it had to intrigue him, set his pulses racing.

She was doing it again now, coming partway across the table, her arms resting on the cloth as she leaned on them. He just wished she'd take the jacket off to give him a better view.

'I wasn't hinting!' she protested, actually managing to sound sincere.

'Of course not.'

His response didn't seem genuine, even in his own ears, but he didn't care. If she thought he didn't believe her, well, tough!

He reached for the bottle in the centre of the table.

'More wine?'

'No, thanks.'

Terrie was beginning to suspect that she'd already had more than enough. The alcohol was warming her blood, which, together with the heat in the room, made her whole body glow uncomfortably. Perhaps she'd feel better without the suit jacket.

'Have you finished your meal?'

He might as well have asked if she could read his mind,

because it seemed she could. No sooner had the thought that he would like her to remove her jacket crossed his mind than she had promptly obliged. And the effect of her actions, the way that her shoulders went back, pushing her small, high breasts forward, the small, sensually wriggling movements she made as she inched the linen sleeves down her arms, was like a neat shot of brandy in his veins, flooding him with heat.

'Yes—thank you. I couldn't eat another thing.'

'Nothing sweet?'

'I'd love something but I don't think my figure could take it.'

The protest was accompanied by a smoothing movement of her hands from her ribcage, down and over her waist.

'Don't tempt me!'

If anyone was *tempting*, then it was her. That gesture had been designed to draw attention to the feminine curves of her shape, the swell of her breasts and the hips that were just barely visible before the flow of the tablecloth covered them. And just the thought of his own hands tracing the path that her fingers had taken made his body clench in cruelly hungry desire.

'Your figure is quite perfect, and you know it.'

He had given up on any attempt to pretend that he was interested in eating. Even the rich red wine was ignored, his half-full glass abandoned, his attention wholly on her.

'You don't have to fish for compliments.'

'I wasn't...'

'Of course not.'

There was something about his smile that caught on her nerves, but she couldn't focus her thinking enough to try and decide just what it was. She felt as if that dark-eyed gaze, his irises more black than brown in the shadowy candlelight, was an intangible force, holding her mesmerised and unable to move.

'But it doesn't matter. You can have all the compliments you want.'

'I—I can?'

His proud head nodded slowly, black eyes locking with grey-blue.

'What would you like me to say? That you are beautiful? Believe me, you are. That your skin has the delicate softness of a perfect peach?'

That he couldn't wait to strip the clinging top from her body, expose the creamy flesh it covered, feast his eyes and his hands, his mouth...?

'That your eyes are the colour of a dove's wing and every bit as—'

'Oh, stop! Stop it!' Terrie cried, mortified into leaning forward and catching hold of his hand in order to shut him up. 'You're going way over the top.'

'You don't believe me?'

Embarrassed beyond speech, she could only shake her head emphatically, sending the pale cloud of hair flying.

'You're flattering—'

'I never flatter.'

His tone stopped her dead, making her blink in confusion.

A single strand of wheat-coloured hair had caught at the corner of her soft pink mouth and, leaning across the table, he reached out and eased it free again. But once he had the silky lock in his hand he didn't release it but lingered, slowly twisting the delicate strands round and round his finger until she was forced to incline her head even closer to him, to avoid him tugging on her scalp.

'Never...' he murmured, his mouth seeming only inches away from her own. And the look in his eyes, the unconcealed passion that burned there, was positively indecent in such a public place.

Twice Terrie swallowed hard, vainly struggling to ease the dryness in her throat. Twice she opened her lips, trying to speak, but no sound would come out.

The rest of the room seemed to have faded into a buzzing haze, the murmured voices of the diners, the faint clatter of plates, the clink of glasses all blurring into one indecipherable mass. But in Terrie's mind, or at least the part of it that would focus, there was only herself and this sensually devastating man before her.

Releasing the pale strand of hair, Gio tucked it back behind her ear with a gentleness that wrenched at something in her heart. And the path that his hand had traced burned against her skin like a mark he had left there, a brand that said she was his and his alone. It would be totally invisible to the naked eye, but she would always know it was there—and so would he.

'Remember that...I never flatter.'

His dark gaze dropped to where her hand still lay on his, looking pale and delicate in contrast to the tanned power of his fingers. Twisting his hand in hers so that they were palm to palm, he linked his fingers with hers, smoothing his thumb softly over her skin.

'So, no sweet,' he said, reverting to the conversation of moments before. 'Coffee? A liqueur?'

'C-coffee would be nice.'

Somehow she forced her tongue to work, wincing inwardly when she heard the way that it croaked and fractured at the end of the sentence.

'We'll take it in the lounge.'

It was a command, not a suggestion, and she could only nod a silent acquiescence to the tone of his voice.

He didn't release her hand as they stood up, but kept

his fingers locked with hers, pulling her to his side as soon as she had moved clear of the table. With his free hand he scooped up the discarded red jacket, tossing it over his arm, barely waiting for her to collect her handbag before he headed towards the door out of the restaurant.

She knew how he felt, Terrie reflected shakenly. She shared that sudden need to be somewhere quieter, less public—more intimate. The thoughts that were in her head, the feelings that his words and his touch had triggered off, were not at all appropriate for the public rooms of a big London hotel. She felt sure that the sensual inferno raging in her blood must be etched onto her face, stamped onto her forehead in letters of fire for all to read. Even if they found the darkest, the most secluded corner of the lounge, she suspected that the heat of the yearning that had her in its grip must radiate from her, scorching anyone who passed.

But if they had wanted peace and quiet, as soon as they entered the lounge she saw that they would be disappointed. The comfortable chairs and cushioned settees dotted around the huge room were all occupied. Almost all the guests who had eaten in the restaurant had chosen to take their coffee here, and they looked as if they planned to linger late into the evening.

'We're out of luck.' Gio's tone was flat, unrevealing of what he was thinking.

Perhaps they were *in* luck. Terrie swallowed, made herself speak before her nerve broke completely.

'Do you think they would bring the coffee to our—to my—your room?'

Such simple words but she almost felt the reverberations that followed from them echoing through the room, making the floor suddenly unsteady beneath her feet. And Gio's sudden silence, the total stillness of his long body beside her, made it clear that he was thinking much the same thing.

'It would be quieter—more private.'

'Is that what you want?'

He was watching her again, waiting for her reply. But all Terrie's strength had deserted her, along with her ability to speak. She could only nod silently, unable to put into words the way she was feeling.

She didn't care if it was foolish, if it was the craziest, the most rash decision she had ever made. Ruthlessly she pushed aside the protesting cries of her offended sense of self-preservation, the promptings of innate caution. It didn't matter what the end result would be, what risks she was running. She only knew that she couldn't let this evening end now, here, in this public room. She couldn't let this man go, walk out of her life, without seeing just how far this unexpected relationship might go.

She knew she would regret it for the rest of her life if she did.

So she nodded again, more firmly this time, and wetted her painfully dry lips, praying that her voice would obey her this time.

'Yes,' she said rawly, thankful that at least she could speak even if the word sounded horribly rough round the edges. 'Yes, that's exactly what I want.'

CHAPTER FOUR

THE lift doors had barely closed before he reached for her.

Terrie could still hear the rumble of the heavy metal moving across the empty space, the sound of the engine starting up, as Gio's hands closed about her arms, pulling her to him. And the slight jolting of the enclosed compartment as it lurched into motion threw her even harder up against his strong frame, her face buried in his shoulder.

'Bellezza... Mia bella...'

The rough sound of his muttered words was blurred by the heavy pounding of his heart under her cheek, a throbbing that was echoed in her own veins as she surrendered willingly to his embrace.

Earlier in the evening she had dreamed, wondered—fantasised—about the way his touch would feel, the sensations that being in his arms might produce. And she hadn't even managed to come close. The reality was so much more—more intense, more sensual, more arousing—more than she had ever imagined it could be.

The heat of his body enclosed her. The scent of his skin was in her nostrils. The sound of his breathing filled her ears at the same time that the warm current of his breath whispered over her sensitive skin, making the delicate nerves tingle all the way down to her toes.

'Teresa...'

Once again that delightful accent turned her name into

something new and exotic, something special only to him, and simply hearing it made her heart turn over in delight.

From the moment that she had made her decision it had been simply a matter of seconds to find a waiter, put in the order for the coffee to be taken to her room.

'Of course, Signor Cardella,' the man had said, clearly knowing only too well just who Gio was. 'Shall I bring it to your suite?'

'No.'

An abrupt shake of his head had emphasised the crispness of his answer.

'To...' Ebony eyes had been turned on Terrie, a question and a prompt combined in the one glance.

'Room five three four.'

Five three four. Her room was on the fifth floor of the hotel, which meant that, even in the speedy, efficient lift, it inevitably took some time to reach their destination.

Some time in which Gio laced his hands around the fine bones of her skull, lifting her face to his, hard fingers massaging her scalp. Time in which his kisses drifted over the surface of her hair, the warmth of his mouth touched her forehead, her closed eyelids, her temples, but never reached her mouth. And most of all time in which the hard, hot pressure of his body revealed forcefully and dramatically the potent power of his desire for her, the swollen force of his erection up against her stomach triggering off a near-delirium of yearning that made her head spin wildly.

'Gio...'

Her fingers clenched in the fine material of his shirt, pulling it loose at his narrow waist. She could no longer wait for the sanctuary of her room and the privacy it would afford them. She wanted to—needed to—touch his skin, feel him properly *now*.

Her hands shook as she ran them up the ridged strength of his ribcage, stroking the warm satin of his skin, brushing across the scattering of crisp hairs that her fingertips encountered. She felt him shudder violently in reaction to her touch and with a muffled curse he rammed her into the far corner of the lift, opposite the door, with her back against the cold metal of the compartment.

His body was against every inch of hers now. Chest to breast, thigh to thigh, his heat and desire crushed into the cradle of her pelvis. And his hands were urgent on her flesh, stroking down her face, along her arms, roughly tugging the white top up to expose more of her skin to his knowing fingers. Moaning aloud, Terrie writhed against his imprisoning strength, throwing her head up and back to allow for more of the hard, snatched kisses that plundered her face and neck.

But still he hadn't kissed her mouth. And she felt that she had never known what it was to feel deprived until this moment, when he continued to deny her that basic intimacy.

'Gio!' she gasped again. 'Gio—kiss me!'

But still his mouth eluded hers. Even though his hands roamed higher and wilder. Even though he caught and cupped the soft swell of her breasts in his hard fingers, sensually tormenting her by rolling her aching nipples in a touch that was such a devastating form of pleasure it came so very near to pain, still he didn't kiss her.

'Gio, damn you! *Please!*'

Driven beyond endurance, she pulled her hands out from under his shirt, hearing something rip faintly as she did so. Ignoring it, she reached up and fastened wildly clutching fingers in the midnight-dark silk of his hair, forcing his head down to meet her own upturned face.

At first she felt his resistance, thought she would never

overcome it, but just when she was convinced that he had won and a faint whimper of defeat almost escaped her, she made one desperate, final effort, and at last his mouth touched hers.

For a second or two Terrie thought she might actually faint in sensual delight. That the warm, firm caress of Gio's lips would actually send her tumbling into an oblivion of pleasure, a world in which nothing mattered but herself and this man and the union between them. But then two things happened at once to jolt her back to the present, reality intruding on her with a jarring shock.

At first she was aware only of Gio's sudden stillness, the swift, disturbing stiffening of his powerful body, the way that his mouth hardened on hers, not in desire, but in a rejection that tore at her heart, slashing a deep wound into it. The other, more mundane event was the creak of the lift, its slowing to a halt, juddering faintly as it reached the fifth floor and stopped.

It was a moment or two before Terrie had collected the composure to realise where they were, drawn in enough breath to mutter, 'I think this is our floor.' And even then she realised that she had recovered well before Gio; that he was not anything like as alert as she had been. When she looked into his face he seemed to be only barely conscious, his eyes glazed and unfocused, two vivid flares of colour scoring along the high, wide cheekbones, his breathing raw and uneven.

'Gio,' she said again carefully, uncertainly. 'We're here. This is my floor.'

Her words invaded his head only slowly, hazily, through the buzzing, burning haze that had invaded his thoughts.

'Sì,' he muttered thickly, his voice still rough with the passion that had taken possession of him. 'Of course.'

Somehow they managed to make their way out of the lift and down the corridor to her room. It seemed that Terrie was as shocked and bewildered by the storm of passion that had assailed them in the lift, certainly if the way that her hand shook when she tried to push her key card into the slot was anything to go by. She tried to manage it twice, failing both times, and on the third attempt actually dropped the card to the floor, giving a cry of frustrated annoyance as she did so.

'Let me.'

Gio stooped, snatched up the card, taking a much-needed moment to draw breath, still his whirling thoughts, before he straightened up again. But even so he was only marginally more successful when he tried to unlock the door, cursing himself under his breath as his hand wavered betrayingly, and having to grip the card tightly as he rammed it into the slot with unnecessary force.

The size of the bedroom was a shock like a blow in the face. Or, rather, the *lack* of size of it. He didn't think he had ever seen such a tiny hotel room in his life.

'*This* is it?' he exclaimed, too stunned to keep the words back. The truth was that he was grateful for some distraction, anything that would divert his mind from the discomfort of his memories of that kiss.

'This is it,' Terrie confirmed, an edge of shaken laughter to her voice. 'What is it, Gio? Are you surprised to see how the other half live?'

'You paid for this!'

'We can't all afford private suites! There is a bathroom...' Terrie added. 'Well—of sorts.'

Flicking on the light to demonstrate, she caught sight of their reflection in the large wall mirror and a muffled gasp that was part horror, part giggle escaped her.

'Would you look at us! Gio—we look... Oh, thank

heaven we didn't meet anyone in the corridor! What would they have thought?'

'That we'd just escaped from a brawl—or an orgy…'

He could only pray that she would take the unevenness of his voice as evidence that he shared her amusement and not as what it really was.

Which was *what*?

If he was honest, then he knew he couldn't actually put a name to the way he was feeling. His emotions were all to pieces, seeming to be on a violent roller coaster plunging down, down, down one moment, only to swing right up again the next.

And all because of one kiss.

Just one kiss.

No. Not 'just' a kiss. Not 'just' anything. It was the first time he had kissed a woman in passion other than his wife.

Dio, the first kiss he had ever known hadn't affected him like this. In fact, the experience had been so long ago, when he was barely in his teens, that the memory had blurred and become so vague that he could hardly remember the girl's name now. But the first time he had kissed Lucia was etched onto his brain, never to be erased. It had felt like coming home; as if all his dreams had finally materialised, centring in the small, delicate shape of the woman he had loved from that moment on.

But *this*. This was so very different. Light-years away from the youthful, innocent experience of the first kiss he had shared with Lucia. It had been a kiss like no other he had ever experienced. And, although he had refused to let it show, it had been a kiss of the fiercest passion he had ever known.

At that first touch of her lips on his, a violent response had seared through him, singeing his nerves, exploding in his brain, making his head swim shockingly. He had known what she wanted, how she had tried to draw his head down to hers, and had set himself to fight against it. And in that first split-second when their mouths had touched the shock had frozen him, held him still. Another heartbeat later and it had all been completely different. Then the fuse that had been lighted at that first contact had burned away, detonating the powder keg of his physical reaction, and blasting his thoughts away with it.

Only the realisation that the lift had come to a halt and Terrie's hasty warning that someone might come had stopped him from making a complete and utter fool of himself.

'The coffee!'

'What?'

He really couldn't take in what Terrie was talking about. If the sight of himself in the mirror, shirt pulled out, tie askew, hair distinctly ruffled, wasn't bad enough, then the sensations throbbing through his body were only aggravating the situation. He still had the taste of her on his lips. The tang of red wine mixed intoxicatingly with the intimate flavour of Terrie herself. He pressed his fingers hard against his mouth, not knowing whether he wanted to rub the back of his hand against his lips to wipe away the taste or hold it, keep it there, lingering, tantalising, arousing, nagging at him with the memory of how he had felt.

And the thought of how very much he wanted to experience it again.

'The coffee?' He shook his dark head slightly, trying to pull himself back into functioning in the present. 'What the hell are you talking about?'

'We ordered coffee,' Terrie reminded him. 'They were

bringing it up to our room. They'll be here any minute. We'd better make ourselves respectable.'

Already she had straightened her top, was reaching for the brush on the dressing table to smooth down her tangled hair. Restoring order and calm where he wanted turmoil and the upheaval of passion, loss of control and the total oblivion of losing his mind to the sensation of ecstasy.

'No.'

It stunned Terrie, stopped her dead, the brush stilling in mid-stroke. Her eyes were wide and startled, clouded with confusion, as she looked up at him.

'What…?' she began but had to swallow the words hastily as she was grabbed, hauled up against him, and they were crushed back down her throat by the sudden violent pressure of his mouth on hers.

And in the blink of an eye her thoughts were swirling again, whirling off into the sensual kaleidoscope of colour and sensation that had assailed her in the lift. She was incapable of thought, wouldn't have cared if a whole army of waiters, laden down with trays of coffee, had marched through her bedroom, gaping openly at every move she made. She was only conscious of this man's touch, this man's lips on hers, the hunger that was thundering in her head, throbbing between her legs—a hunger that he had created and only he could appease.

This time his mouth was a devastating combination of hard and soft, starting off fiercely demanding and then suddenly and unexpectedly gentling into an enticing sweetness that eased open her lips, allowing him more intimate access to her mouth. The play of his tongue was an erotic caress, and the tangle of his hands in her hair, holding her exactly where he wanted and at what angle, was an arousing indication of his strength and the ease with which he could use it either to excite or control.

Her own hands went up, her fingers closing over the hard muscles of his shoulders and clinging, needing the support because her legs were unsteady beneath her, suddenly feeling as if they were made of nothing but cotton wool. She was lost, adrift on a heated sea of sensation, and could only abandon herself to the waves and the direction they wanted to take her.

The rap at the door she had been anticipating came while her heart was still pounding, so that for a second she was only aware of it as another, sharper, note in the crescendo of passion that was building inside her. But then it was repeated and at the same moment another sound blended with it, a shrill, higher pitched note that intruded into the moment, disrupting the mood.

Against her lips, Gio muttered something dark and furious in rough Italian. But when the summons came again he moved sharply, releasing Terrie abruptly and turning towards the door.

Abandoned so unexpectedly, she found herself staggering for a moment before dropping down awkwardly onto the bed, unable to remain standing. Her eyes were hazed, barely focused as she watched Gio cross the room in two swift strides, pull open the door with one hand, while hunting in his pocket for his phone with the other.

She was still trying to collect her thoughts as he waved an autocratic gesture towards the coffee-table, indicating that the tray of coffee-pot and cups should be placed there, pushed an obviously generous tip into the waiter's hand, and ushered him back out the door all in one fluid movement. And then he turned his attention to the still-ringing phone.

'Scusi... Sì?'

Whoever was on the phone was someone he wanted to talk to, Terrie reflected, stunned by the sudden transformation of his face. The hard lines and planes seemed to soften. Between the thick black lashes she could see a new light in the deep, dark eyes, and a dancing little smile curled the hard line of his mouth into something that made her heart kick sharply, stealing her breath away.

The conversation was in Italian too fast and too accented for her to be able to catch any more than a single word here or there. But there was one word she did hear, and it stuck in her mind like a burr, stinging sharply.

Cara, he said, his tone warming and gentling. *Cara mia.* And the words were like a hard, brutal slap in her face, cold as ice after the heat of her reaction just moments earlier.

Once more her eyes fastened on Gio's face, watching, reinterpreting the new expression on his face. The sense of devastation in the pit of her stomach, the feeling of being so close to something very sweet and very special, only to have it snatched right away from her, was like a raw bruise, aching and sore.

'*Buona notte,*' Gio finished. '*Ben dorme.*'

She couldn't wait until he had put the phone away.

'Are you married?'

It froze him in the middle of closing the case.

'Married?'

There was something disturbing in the way that he had reacted, the look in his eyes. Something that set her heart racing, jolting unevenly in distress.

'I heard you! You called—you said *"cara"*. I might not understand much Italian, but I do know that word and I know what it means! *Cara*—darling—*darling!*' she repeated emphatically when he simply sat there, dark eyes unreadable. 'Who were you calling *darling?*'

'Is it any of your...?'

The silver phone case closed with a dangerous snap and Gio obviously changed his mind about what he had been about to say.

'My sister-in-law,' he conceded unexpectedly, but the words were still coldly clipped, falling like shards of ice into the rapidly cooling atmosphere. 'Signora Megan Santorino. The wife of my half-brother Cesare. You don't believe me? Here...'

The phone was tossed down onto the bed, sliding across the blue and white bedspread to just within reach of Terrie's fingers.

'Ring back—hear for yourself. The redial button is—'

'I don't need the redial button!' Terrie spat, painfully embarrassed by unnecessary instruction, the over-elaborate pretence at concern for her to get it right. 'I don't need to ring back! I—I believe you!'

How could she think anything else when she saw the flaring fury in his eyes, the tension that held his long body taut? She'd blundered badly somewhere.

'Gio—I believe you. Please—I'm sorry. Forgive me.'

For the space of several distinctly uneven heartbeats, he simply glared into her eyes, his jaw set tight, his mouth clamped into a thin line. But then at last, to her infinite relief, he raked both hands through the raven darkness of his hair and nodded slowly.

'OK,' he said, his tone losing just a touch of that attacking quality. 'Fine.'

And that was it? Terrie wondered. Topic closed? Continue as before? She didn't know if she could.

The sharply heated little exchange had taught her something. A lesson she had more than needed. It had shown her just how little she knew about this man, other than the most basic facts.

It had also revealed another side to Gio Cardella. A very different, very disturbing side that was in total contrast to the urbane, courteous, charming man who had been her dinner companion this evening. It had shown her Giovanni Cardella, the hotshot international lawyer, the man who had been in court today prosecuting an important fraud case—and won. In those few, unnervingly uncomfortable moments she had come up against Giovanni Cardella, counsel for the prosecution—and quite frankly it had unnerved her.

'She's seven months pregnant.'

The comment caught her unawares, all the more so because of the casually conversational way that Gio delivered it. It was as if the disturbing confrontation hadn't happened, or he had dismissed it from his mind at once.

'Who?'

'Megan. She's expecting her first baby in May and she's already as big as a house. She rang to complain about the heat.'

'The heat!'

Terrie's eyes went to the windows beyond which, with the typical unreliability of an English spring, the rain had suddenly started to fall, great drops darkening the paving stones in the courtyard outside.

'Sicily has a very different climate from England.'

'Of—of course.'

The trace of amusement warming his voice was her undoing. She could feel it heating the blood in her veins, making it throb its way around her body. And if she glanced up she could see the way that a hint of laughter had lit up his eyes, melting the ice that had been in them moments before.

And she wanted that. Needed that change of mood. Because, terrifying as she found it to admit, she now realised

that in the few short hours since she had met Giovanni
Cardella things had moved on at a pace that she had neither anticipated nor, if she was honest, genuinely wanted.
She wouldn't have believed it possible, but she was already in so deep that it was going to devastate her if she
had to back out now.

Or if Gio left her in anger, or some foolish mistake on
her part drove him away from her.

'Well, they brought the coffee,' Gio muttered drily.

His gesture indicated the tray on the table, the fine
china cups and saucers, the silver coffee-pot. The waiter
had brought brandy too, the amber-coloured liquid glow-
ing fierily in delicate crystal balloon glasses.

'So do you *want* coffee, Teresa?'

She was thrilled to hear a new softness in his voice, the
husky note of invitation that held the promise of a future,
a beginning, rather than an end.

'No,' she whispered, her voice very low but firm with
conviction. 'I can't say I do.'

What she *did* want was clear in her eyes, written deep
in the clouded pools of her irises, burning in the appre-
hensive but unwavering gaze she turned on his dark,
watchful face.

Gio drew in a long, deep, faintly ragged breath and
nodded slowly. And when he moved it was to hold out
his arm, his hand slightly curved to beckon her to him.

'Then come here,' he said sharply, huskily, the musical
intonation of his accent deepening on each word he spoke.
'Come here to me, *belleza*, and let's finish what we've
started.'

CHAPTER FIVE

'COME here...and let's finish what we've started.'

Gio found that his words echoed inside his head as he watched Terrie lever herself up off the bed and then stand, hesitating, clearly undecided whether to obey him or not.

Finish what we've started.

What *had* they started? And, more to the point, how was it going to end? Was he going to be able to leave it as the one-night stand he had planned on, the 'fun' that Terrie had indicated she wanted? He didn't know and quite frankly at this moment he simply didn't care.

Tomorrow morning he might be able to walk away without a backward glance. He might be happy to say goodbye and let her go out of his life without a second thought; he didn't know. The only certainty in his mind was that *now* he couldn't do any such thing. He couldn't leave not having made love to this woman. He couldn't go without having known the full experience of sleeping with her, having her, of seeing whether the reality of her lived up to the fantasy, the promise, the hunger that her kisses had awoken in him.

After two long years of shutting away his sexual feelings, keeping them out of his life with a blockade of loneliness and working until he dropped from sheer exhaustion, it now seemed that the dam had been breached. The barriers were down once and for all and the floodtide of sensations could not be held back. Instead it was flowing fierce and wild and free, sweeping aside all restraint, all trace of anything like thought or hesitation or self-control.

He wanted this tonight; and for tonight at least he was going to have it.

'Teresa?'

She would have travelled far further and overcome far greater obstacles if it meant that she could hear him use her name in that soft, that tender way. But even so, the short distance across the deep blue carpet to where Gio stood, still with his hand outstretched, seemed to take an age. Forever.

She could hardly make her feet move. Her legs had no strength at all beneath her, and she could only step hesitantly and uncertainly, her eyes fixed on his face.

But in his face she found her strength. In those deep, dark eyes, so intently fixed on her, was all the encouragement she needed. He was there for her, and that was all that mattered, all that she wanted.

This was just a beginning. It was stepping out into the unknown, and that needed courage. She didn't know what might happen days down the line; she only knew that for now she had to close her eyes and jump, and take it on trust that he wouldn't let her fall.

And as it had been in the lift, so now his arms were there, ready and waiting for her. They gathered her close, collected her in, and drew her up to him. And when she lifted her face to him his mouth came down on hers, hard and hot and hungry and passionate. It crushed her own mouth open, parting it to the sweep of his tongue, the deepening of the caress.

And she gave herself up to that caress openly and willingly, all trace of hesitation gone, all fear swept aside in the floodtide of passionate hunger that took possession of her. She couldn't get close enough, couldn't feel enough of him pressed up against her, her senses swooning in intoxication as she inhaled the clean, potent scent of his body and felt its heat surround her.

Hard hands tangled in her hair, twisting the fine blonde strands around the long, tanned fingers, holding her head exactly where he wanted it so that he could kiss her in just the way that he wanted. And what he wanted was what she wanted too. All that she wanted was here in this one small room. The rest of the world, the past, the worries of the future, all faded away into an indecipherable blur. There was only the present and this man and the flames they had lit between them.

And those flames had her totally in their grip now. They were licking along every nerve, searing every inch of skin. Gio seemed to sense unerringly just what she was feeling and where as he freed his right hand from her hair, leaving the other one to hold her head captive, and let his other hand roam wilfully over her body. Somehow he touched unerringly on every most sensitive spot, every yearning pleasure point that pulsed just below the surface of her flesh. And in the same instant that his touch appeased one hunger, it also awoke another, deeper, more primitive one. One that demanded a satisfaction as wild and potent and as primal as its own forceful nature.

'Gio…'

His name was a muttered sound of encouragement mixed with protest on her lips. She wanted more than this exploratory touch on her body, through her clothes. She wanted the feel of his hands on her skin, the warmth of flesh on flesh. She wanted to feel his hands demand, and her body respond. Every inch, every sense, every nerve rising to meet this, the most basic claim of all that a man could make on a woman.

'Gio…'

And yet at the same time she wanted to prolong this

moment into infinity. She wanted this first coming together to go on and on forever. For a lifetime. Because
only a lifetime would be long enough for her to fully
experience, to fully *know* this first stage of making love
with Giovanni Cardella.

Never again would it be so new, so unknown, so *fresh*.
And she wanted to linger in that freshness, even as some
deeper, inner claim of her female nature was throbbing
hard and wild at the joining of her legs. And much as she
wanted to delay, to savour, to enjoy, she knew that that
demand would soon grow too strong to be ignored. It
would have to be appeased or it would tear her apart.

'Oh, Gio...'

This time the impatience was uppermost in her tone,
and in the moment of hearing it she also felt Gio's silent
laughter against her face.

'*Calma, bella mia. Calma,*' he whispered into her
mouth. 'We have all night.'

But even as he said the words, he knew that they were
a lie. There was no way that he could wait, or delay this
much longer. It was the difference that had kept him on
a tight rein so far—the stunning, shocking differences between the woman in his arms and the wife he had made
love to before. The only woman in his life for so many
years.

And the differences had seemed so important in the first
moments that he had touched her. The colour and length
of her hair. The pale cloud of blonde that fell around her
face and shoulders where Lucia's had been short and dark.
The long, slender limbs; the way her face was so much
closer to his when she stood next to him. The intensely
personal scent of her skin.

In those first seconds of touching her, holding her, she
seemed so very, very different. And the kick that his

senses gave, the way that his heart clenched painfully, made him wonder, just for an instant, whether he could go through with this. But then Terrie stirred against him, and he knew that his mind, his senses, were no longer in the past. That what mattered was here and now.

And she was here, now.

And she was what he wanted.

What he desired—so much.

And so he kissed her again, losing himself in the feel of her lush mouth beneath his. The warm, moist delicacy of her kiss seemed to melt his bones, turning his blood to white heat in his veins. He wanted to rush, to grab and snatch at the pleasure offered, yet at the same moment he wanted to delay, to linger and stretch it out as long as possible.

He wished that her white top had button fastenings. The thought of the slow, sensual delight of slipping each one through its hole, sliding apart the two delicate sides of the garment, appealed to his sense of anticipation, the thrill of waiting, building excitement on excitement. But in the moment that he tugged the stretchy cotton up and over her head, his fingers brushing over the heated skin of her torso, his already hungrily aroused body hardened and tightened even more. His hopes of delaying, of waiting flew out the window in the space of a heartbeat. And as he looked down onto the soft, creamy mounds of her breasts, lifted and displayed in voluptuous enticement by the silk and lace of her pale pink bra, he knew that he was lost.

'Teresa,' he muttered, his voice raw and thick with desire. *'Teresa, cara mia, bella mia...'*

Terrie was lost in sensation, and the sound of Gio's voice, the exotic traces of his accent deepened and roughened by the passion that burned deep in his eyes, made her shiver with excited anticipation. The stroke of his hands over her upper body, the fine lines of her ribcage, made her writhe in uncontrolled response. But the moment when those knowing fingers trailed upwards, drifted for sweet, tormenting moments over the silk of her bra, awakening the sensitive flesh beneath, made her freeze in sudden delighted anticipation, her breath catching sharply in her throat.

That felt *so* good. And it set up a stinging, burning response of hunger that radiated throughout her body, centring in a molten pool at the junction of her legs.

'I want this...' she muttered, her voice almost as rough as his. 'Gio...I *want*...'

The sound of his slightly shaken laughter filled the space where the words had deserted her and she felt the hot pressure of his mouth on her, and then again on her cheekbone, the delicate pulse at her temple.

'Do you think I don't know that, *angelina*?' he muttered against her skin. 'I know what you want—and you will get it...'

Once more he kissed her softly, his hands stilling on her breasts, and a whimper of frustrated protest escaped her lips at his abandonment of the cruelly arousing caresses.

'Don't...' she began, only to have her mouth captured again, the words of complaint pushed back down her throat.

'I know what you want, *cara*,' he repeated huskily. 'It is what I want too. But I am trying to be considerate here.'

'Con...siderate?'

It was the last thing she had expected.

'I want to take this steady—make it good for you...'

There was a raw edge to the words that made it sound as if his control was unravelling fast, his ability to keep himself on a tight rein slipping away from him. The pulse of electrical excitement that shot through her in response made her shift against him sharply, the swell of her pelvis coming up hard against the heated shaft of his erection.

Gio's breath hissed in sharply through his clenched teeth and one hand dropped from her breast to cup and hold her bottom, crushing her into even closer contact with the potent sign of his arousal.

'But if you keep rubbing yourself up against me like that, then steady is not what I can be.'

'And did I ask for *steady*?'

Terrie's mouth formed into a mock-pout, smoky eyes gleaming provocatively as she looked up into his tense face.

'Did I ask for consideration? Did I—?'

The end of her question vanished into a gasp of unexpected delight as she was grabbed, hauled into his arms, and lifted high into the air.

'No consideration, huh?'

He swung her over towards the bed, dropping her down onto the mattress with a suddenness that brought the breath from her lungs in an 'oof' of surprise.

'No steadiness…'

He was down beside her before she had recovered her breath, taking her mouth again in an almost brutal, searing kiss.

'You asked for it, lady…'

Hands as restless as his voice tugged the delicate straps of her bra down, imprisoning her arms against her sides in the same moment that he exposed the tender flesh of her breasts. His mouth took the sensitive skin by storm, kissing, licking, even nibbling gently, along the creamy curves until he reached the swollen pink nipple. When the heat of his lips closed over the aching bud and he suckled hard, Terrie felt that she would swoon with the torment of the blend of pleasure and pain that laid siege to every nerve in her body.

'Gio—oh, *Gio*…!'

His name was an incoherent litany of need and submission, tumbling from her lips in the same moment that her hands communicated another, very different mood. Urgent and demanding, they wrenched at the buttons on his shirt, tugging them apart in a flurry of hungry need.

Gio helped her by shrugging the fine linen from his shoulders, tossing the discarded garment to the floor before turning his attention to the now rumpled and disordered skirt that was pushed up around her slender hips.

'*Stockings,*' he growled on a note of purely predatory satisfaction as his efficient actions exposed the delicate lacy tops that clung to her pale thighs. 'Do you know what stockings do to me?'

Terrie could only shake her head, sending her blonde hair flying in a wheat-coloured halo. She didn't know, but she could certainly guess. And the rough, crooning sound he made low in his throat, the fierce glitter of his eyes, the raw unevenness of his breathing told their own tale.

The one flimsy barrier between him and the hot, moist centre of her need of him was easily stripped away. Clever, knowing fingers found just the right spot and stroked, caressed, tormented until she was gasping for breath, head tossing on the pillows, her own hands clenching over the hard muscles in his shoulders and clinging on desperately for support.

'*Gio!*'

'I know, *cara.* I know…'

Between them they disposed of his remaining clothing, the sensation of heated skin against skin adding further fuel to the inferno already raging in every sensitised inch of Terrie's body. She was so close now—so close to the moment of ultimate union, ultimate intimacy, that she couldn't bear to wait. And when he seemed to hesitate, just for a second, she almost panicked, clutching at him and bringing him closer to her, only now aware of how he had momentarily backed away.

'Teresa...'

Her name was a moan of protest on his lips.

'I have—nothing... Do you...?'

She didn't understand what he was saying. Couldn't understand why he had hesitated. Didn't *want* him to pause, to think, to do *anything* now but take her, love her, make her his.

'No, no, no,' she muttered. 'It doesn't matter—really, it's not important, not... Gio—*please!*'

The final word was a cry of desperation, of longing. And in the same moment that she let it escape her she lifted her hips from the bed, pressing herself invitingly against him, mutely encouraging his final possession.

Through the roaring in her head she heard Gio give a faint sigh of surrender, sensed all resistance seep from him like air from a punctured balloon. And the next moment he had curved hard, hot hands around her hips, holding her just where he wanted her as he thrust his powerful body into hers in one long, forceful movement.

Almost immediately whatever control he had been exerting broke totally. His movements, hard and fast and fierce, took possession of her, took control of her, lifting her up and up, riding the waves of demanding passion, cresting each one. Going higher and higher and higher...until there was nowhere else to go but over the edge into an explosion of ecstasy and oblivion that totally engulfed them both.

*   *   *

It was the first, faint fingers of light from the dawn that crept through the uncurtained window and fell onto his face that gradually penetrated the heavy, exhausted sleep into which Gio had fallen, making him stir and frown slightly, wondering where he was.

Outside in the street below, the sound of cars, a noise that never stopped in this city that never seemed to sleep, reminded him that he was in London. But this was not his room. Not the elegant suite he had woken in every other morning of his stay...

Even as his thoughts were sorting and deciphering the information, a small, soft sigh, like the murmur of a sleeping kitten, broke through his confusion, waking him fully and sharply.

Teresa.

Memory hit home with the force of a lethal bullet, driving away the last traces of sleep and blasting him awake in a moment of pure shock.

Teresa. *Terrie.* The woman called herself Terrie.

She had told him her surname, but it hadn't registered in his mind. To him she was just Teresa. Nothing more.

The woman whose bed he had shared all night long. The woman whose body had opened to him, welcomed him in. And in whose arms he had lost himself, forgotten, for a few hours at least, the loneliness and emptiness of his life. With her he had shared a blazing passion that had somehow made him hungry in the very same moment that it had satisfied him. He hadn't been able to sleep, had known no rest, until he had taken her again and again and again, in an exhausting outpouring of need that he hadn't believed he would ever experience again. In her bed he had found the oblivion he had been looking for. And in this woman he had found some of the deepest, most sensual satisfaction he had ever experienced.

The woman with whom he had betrayed the memory of his beloved wife.

'Oh, Lucia!'

With an effort he swallowed down the groan of pain and guilt that almost escaped his lips, clamping his mouth tight shut against it. Beside him Terrie sighed again and nestled deeper into the pillows, the long, tangled mane of her hair obscuring her face from his sight.

Levering himself up onto his side, Gio rested his weight on one elbow as he turned to study her sleeping form. His fingers itched to sweep the blonde locks away from her face and expose the delicate cheekbones, the full softness of her mouth, but caution and common sense warned him sharply to hold back. To touch her was to risk waking her. And waking her would have the sort of consequences he wasn't prepared to risk.

If she woke then he would be tempted all over again. If she stirred, turned to him, still warm and relaxed from sleep, then he would want her with the hunger that was still lingering just below the surface of his mind, the raw passion that had had him in its grip all through the night.

'If she *wakes*…!' he muttered, low and rough. '*If*… Oh, *Madre de Dio*!' Who was he trying to fool?

He wasn't even convincing himself. Even as the thoughts crossed his mind, his body was waking, hardening in savagely demanding response simply to her closeness, to the warmth of her skin reaching his, the scent of her flesh coiling round his senses like a drug.

Face facts, he told himself with furious reproach. He wanted her again. Even the passion-soaked night that they had shared had done nothing to appease his clamouring senses. If anything he was hungrier than before. He wanted her, and he wanted her *now*, with a yearning that all the guilt and the regret could do nothing to suppress.

'Inferno!' he swore savagely under his breath, throwing back the bedclothes and pushing himself from the bed, careless of whether he disturbed the sleeping woman or not.

But it seemed that she was even more exhausted than he had been. For an instant she stirred slightly, seeming to sense his movement away from her side. But the next moment she had cuddled down again, once more giving that gentle sigh that tugged at something in his heart.

No! He wouldn't let her reach him, touch him again, either physically or mentally. One night he had told himself. One night and that was all. There was no room in his life for anything more.

His clothes were scattered all around the room—the shirt hanging half on and half off a chair, his trousers in an appallingly crumpled heap on the blue patterned carpet. Brown eyes clouding in disbelief and distaste, he forced himself to collect them up, shake them out into some sort of order at least.

What he really longed for was a shower. A long, hot, ruthlessly scouring shower.

Or did he mean a long, cold, ruthlessly icy one? The sort of shower that might just suppress the wanton longings that his weakened flesh was still subjected to. That would freeze his molten blood so effectively it would leave him shuddering and gasping in total shock.

Because it seemed that only that would drive away the lingering memories of the pleasures of this woman's body, erase the knowledge of how it had felt to possess her soft femininity, destroy the longing to experience it all over again.

But a shower was a risk he couldn't take. The sound of the rushing water would wake the sleeping Terrie. She would stir, and, finding him gone, his side of the bed empty and cold, would come in search of him. And if she found him in the shower...

'*Dio*, no!'

The thudding of his heart set the blood throbbing inside his skull, blotting out the possibility of rational thought. Just to imagine himself and Terrie close together in the shower cubicle, naked and relaxed, the flow of the warm water over already heated skin, was more than he could endure. Unable to withstand the beguilingly erotic pictures that were flooding through his mind, he snatched up his disordered clothing and escaped into the bathroom, shutting the door behind him as firmly as the need for quiet allowed.

Dear God, but he looked like hell!

The man who stared back at him from the mirror over the basin had heavy, hooded eyes with deep, dark shadows underneath them. His jawline was rough with a night's growth of beard, and his hair was in wild disorder, making him remember Terrie's urgent, clutching fingers closing over his scalp as her orgasm shook her slender body in wave after wave of ecstasy.

'No!'

He must stop thinking like that. Must stop remembering.

Bending over the sink, he ran the cold tap until the water was icy and then scooped it up into his hands, splashing it fiercely into his still sleep-softened face. He had to wake up. Had to get out of here as he had always planned.

By the time he had dried his face, pulled on his clothes, and forced his wayward hair into some degree of order again, he felt much more awake. Awake and in control of himself at last. Ready to return to the way of life that had been the norm before the blonde land-mine that was

Teresa Something had exploded right in his face, throwing him totally off balance.

She was still asleep when he made his way back into the bedroom. Still lying on her side, slightly curled up into a vulnerable ball, her face still hidden by the pale mass of her hair.

He could leave now. He could get out of here, get away before she even surfaced, and she would never know. He could simply walk out that door and...

But even as he thought it, he knew he could never act on the impulse. Their time together was over and, even though his greedy body was urging him to have second, and even third thoughts about the decision he had made, he was determined to stick with his resolve. But he couldn't just walk out the door without a word. He'd have to stay and say something to her. Even if that something was only goodbye.

With a sigh he flung himself into the room's single chair, raking both his hands through his newly smoothed hair, ruffling it into total disorder once again. If it had to be done then he wished she would wake. She was just too tempting lying there, sleeping. Too innocent. Too vulnerable.

Too watchable.

Some sound he had made must have disturbed her, penetrating at last the deep, deep sleep that had her in its grip. As he watched, he saw her stir, saw the faint change in her breathing as she swam to the surface of her consciousness. She stretched slightly, tensed a little as she felt the space beside her, and then turned over, her hand going out to where she had expected him to be.

'Gio?'

It was a sleepy little murmur, softly puzzled, only halfway conscious.

'Gio?'

He watched in silence as she blinked, frowned, half opened her eyes, then let them drift shut again as if rousing herself was just too much effort.

He knew exactly how she felt. Knew that heavy, almost drugged sense of disorientation on waking to find that nothing was quite as you expected it. That the scene you had anticipated finding had altered subtly and disturbingly.

'Gio?'

This time she came round more fully. Lifting her head from the pillow, she peered, puzzled, at the vacant side of the bed, her light brown brows drawing together in a frown of incomprehension, her lavender gaze still slightly unfocused.

'Where…?'

'Here,' he inserted quickly, drawing her eyes to where he sat with his back to the window. 'I'm here.'

'Oh, yes. There you are!'

To his horror she smiled straight at him. A smile that was still clouded by sleep, that made her already gentle expression even softer, twisting something that felt painfully like regret deep inside.

'What are you doing there? And why are you dressed? Do you have somewhere to go?'

'No—nowhere important.'

'Good.'

The smile grew, and so did his discomfort.

'In that case, take those clothes off again and come back to bed.'

'That won't be possible.'

The words were clipped and curt, cold as ice.

'Won't be…?'

Her confusion made her look even more vulnerable, even more young and childlike and...

'Teresa, don't! Stop it right now.'

'Stop what? Don't what?'

'Don't *look* like that! Don't look at me like that. Oh, hell, *belleza*...'

Once more he raked impatient fingers through his hair, the gesture more expressive of his unease even than the ragged edge to his voice.

'How in God's name am I supposed to leave you when you look at me like that?'

CHAPTER SIX

LEAVE you.

How am I supposed to leave you?

The words didn't make any sense to Terrie's still sleep-fuddled brain. What was Gio talking about?

She had finally fallen into a deep sleep of total exhaustion at some point well into the early hours of the morning. For some hours her oblivion had been absolute, but then, slowly and gradually, she had come awake. And, stirring slightly under the soft quilted duvet, she had felt the faint stiffness in her limbs, the tiny aches and bruises that reminded her instantly of how she had spent so much of the night.

And she had smiled to herself at the memories.

She had never woken to so good a feeling before. Never felt so totally satisfied, so relaxed, so deeply, contentedly at one with the world. Last night she had met a very special man, and she had spent a deliriously sensual, a gloriously happy night with him.

And she was firmly convinced that, after such a special night, today could only be the start of a whole new life. A life that she hoped, prayed, dreamed would include the presence of Giovanni Cardella in it for a long, long time.

On that thought she had stirred, swimming up slowly, close to the surface of waking. And in that state she had reached out a hand to the spot where, as sleep had finally closed over her, the warm, vital, wonderful body of Gio had been lying, satiated and relaxed at her side.

Which was when the first tiny flaw had entered the

perfect beginning to her day. The space was empty, the sheets already cooling rapidly as if the man who had slept there had been gone for some time.

'Gio?'

Frowning faintly, she had stirred again, struggling to make herself wake up a little more.

'Here…' She heard his voice, coming vaguely to her through the thick, clinging strands of sleep as she forced her eyes open.

He was sitting in the chair, with his back to the window. His head was silhouetted against the faint grey light, his face half in shadow as a result. What she could see looked wonderful. More than wonderful.

He no longer had the sleek, groomed perfection of the night before. His hair was only partly combed, his cheeks and jaw unshaven, roughened with the dark shadow of stubble. His eyes were heavy and hooded, and his clothes were only pulled on, some buttons still not fastened, his shirt only roughly pushed into the waistband of the grey trousers.

But in Terrie's mind he looked all the more wonderful because of that. Because she knew what had put that sleepily sensual look into his eyes. Whose hands had ruffled the sleek, jet-black perfection of his hair. The memories of the night they had shared still coloured everything in a rich, golden glow, so she was incapable of seeing anything wrong in it.

But a couple of moments later, as each unexpectedly cool response to her attempts to entice him back into her bed fell onto her exposed nerves like icy drops of rain, she was forced into a radical and uncomfortable rethink.

'Gio, what do you mean? Why are you leaving? Where are you going?'

The suspicion and the fear that had her heart in an icy

grip began to deepen when he didn't answer, but simply sat there, dark eyes levelled on her face. With a struggle she forced herself to wake properly, rousing herself to open her eyes, pull herself upright on her pillows.

A second later, a hasty, instinctive rethink had her pulling the covers up too, covering her exposed shoulders and breasts. Still not entirely sure why, she only knew she felt too exposed, too vulnerable like that.

'Wh-when are you coming back?'

'Never.' It was cold and flat and totally unyielding.

'Never? But why? What have I done…?'

'It's not what you've done, Teresa. It's what I didn't do. Or, rather, what I didn't say.'

'I don't understand.'

He was speaking in riddles, making her mind whirl in confusion. But all the same her blood ran cold simply at the sound of his words, her heart filling with dread at the prospect of what might be to come.

'I never said there would be any tomorrow. Or any sort of future, come to that. I never promised you anything beyond one night. We had that night. Now it's time to say goodbye.'

'But…'

Terrie's eyes would not focus and when she looked at his face it was just a blur. Blinking hard, she forced them back into clarity and immediately wished she hadn't. She had seen more emotion on the carved stone face of the Sphinx, and her blood ran so cold in fear that she shivered in spite of the cosy quilt.

'Goodbye?' It was just a low, desolate murmur.

'Goodbye.'

To her horror she realised that he had taken it as agreement. As if she was saying farewell to him.

And it seemed that that was exactly what he wanted.

He was getting to his feet, reaching for his shoes, stamping his feet into them.

He truly hadn't expected it to be quite that easy, Gio reflected thankfully. She must have known it was coming, but all the same he had anticipated some sort of protest, a touch of complaint at her swift dismissal. She *had* tried to cajole him back into bed at first, he recalled, thankful that the need to fasten his shoes meant he had to bend his head, so avoiding looking into her face, and hiding his own expression from her.

If she tried again he wasn't totally sure he would be able to resist her. He hadn't been prepared for how difficult it had been the first time. The struggle he had had with his most basic instincts not to toss off his clothes again, fling back the covers and join her once more in the indolent warmth of the big double bed. Even now, in spite of the fact that he couldn't see her, his body was recalling the sensual delights of the night, hardening in nagging demand and yearning for a repeat indulgence. The clutch of hunger deep in his gut made his hands disturbingly unsteady on his laces.

The sooner he was out of here the better. All he had to do was to get out the door—close it between them...

'No!'

The cry came unexpectedly, shocking him into stillness just as he caught up his jacket from the chair.

'*Che?*'

'I said no!'

Terrie didn't know what had brought this on; what had made him suddenly so determined to leave. She only knew that she wasn't going to stand by and let it happen.

Launching herself out of the bed, heedless now of her total nudity, she flung herself at Gio as he turned towards the door. His arm was beyond her reach, no matter how hard she stretched, but she did manage to catch hold of his trailing jacket, her fingers tangling in the fine material and clutching hard.

'You're not going anywhere!'

Her gasping protest, and the sudden catch on his jacket forced Gio to halt abruptly. Whirling round, he directed a furious glare into her uneasy face. One that shook her right to the roots of her soul and almost had her releasing her hold on the jacket again, fearful of possible retribution.

But a moment later she had collected herself, drawing in some sort of courage with the rough, unsteady breath that she struggled for.

'You're not going,' she repeated stubbornly. 'Not without some sort of explanation.'

If that glare had been terrible, then the look of pure contempt that raked her from the dishevelled, tangled cloud of blonde hair and down over every exposed and vulnerable inch of her naked body was even worse. It seemed to scour her sensitive skin, stripping away a vital protective layer, and leaving her raw and bleeding, emotionally if not actually physically.

'And who,' he enquired in tones of pure ice, 'is going to stop me?'

'I am...'

She had to force herself to say it, but somehow the fact that it came out through closely gritted teeth as she tightened her uncertain grip on the jacket seemed to give the words an added force, a determination that she was far from actually feeling.

'Oh, are you?'

It was even more condescending than before and the arrogant look that he directed at her down the long, straight line of his nose threatened to shrivel her into ashes right where she stood. It took every ounce of courage to stay where she was, though her toes curled in nervous reaction, digging into the soft pile of the carpet.

'*Sì?*'

The softness of the question took her almost by surprise so that she was unprepared for his sudden movement as he tried to snatch his coat away from her briefly loosened grasp. But she managed to grab at it just in time, setting up a brief and ungainly contest as each of them fought for possession of the item.

'Teresa...'

Never before had she heard her name spoken with such ferocity, such venom.

'You will rip my jacket.'

'No, you will!' she flung at him defiantly. 'But only if you keep up this ridiculous tug of war. Oh, come on, Gio...is it asking so much? Just tell me why...'

He drew himself up, taller, darker and more imposing than ever before. Dangerously so.

'I don't have to explain myself to you.'

He exerted a little extra force, pulling the jacket a few inches nearer to his side.

'And I say you do!'

With a rough little movement she tugged it right back.

For a couple of moments the garment seesawed between them, then with one final jerk Gio wrenched it out of her hands and fully into his. But Terrie barely saw it go. The movement had jolted the jacket roughly, shaking a couple of items free from the pockets, one of them a black leather wallet. And as she watched, fascinated, it tumbled to the ground, landing with a faint, soft thud, and falling open right at her feet.

'*Inferno!*'

With barely half her mind she was aware of Gio's furious curse, his dart forwards, his hand coming out. But that was enough for instinct to come into play, warning her that something was wrong. Something he didn't want her to see or know about.

Totally abandoning the disputed jacket, she turned her attention instead to the wallet, grabbing it up in the same swift movement that took her partway across the room, and into the comparative safety of the other side of the bed.

'Teresa!'

Her name was both a threat and a warning.

'Give that back to me—now!'

'No chance...'

She wanted to defy him totally. To challenge him to do something about her actions. But her mind chose just that most inopportune moment to push her into glancing across the room, catching sight of her reflection in the mirror on the front of the wardrobe.

It was just the wrong time to bring home to her the fact that she was totally naked, her pale skin faintly flushed from her recent exertions.

'Oh, no!'

Horrified beyond embarrassment, she clasped her arms across her exposed breasts, whirling in a frantic circle as she hunted for, found and yanked on her pale pink towelling robe, forcing the hand that held the wallet down the sleeve. It was impossible to fasten the tie belt, so she had to content herself with pulling the two sides together, clutching them close to cover as much as possible.

'Teresa... Give me back that wallet!'

'Wrong move, Gio! If you'd really wanted me to give it back without looking, then you should have pretended it just wasn't important! All you've done is to pique my curiosity. Now, let me see...'

One-handed, she caught the wallet by a corner, shook it over the rumpled bed, watching as several items fell out and tumbled down onto the quilt.

Credit and cheque cards, some English notes, and others she supposed must be Italian lira, a book of stamps...some photographs.

And in an instant, without needing to think or to ask questions, she knew that the photographs were what he had wanted to hide from her. They fell in a bundle, some totally hidden, others partly exposed, and as they did so one single, harshly explosive curse broke from Gio's lips. But when Terrie glanced up at him, suspicion in her eyes, he made no further move to stop her. Instead, he lifted both his hands, flinging them outwards in a supremely Italian gesture of defeat.

'Be my guest...' The ironical inflexion he gave the words was so sharp, so bitter that Terrie actually flinched as it stung like the lash of a whip.

Well, what did it matter now? Gio asked himself. What did any of it matter?

He didn't even know why he'd been so determined that she shouldn't find out. Why it had mattered so much that she didn't discover the truth about Lucia. About his wife.

No. Even as he formed the thought, he realised that that wasn't the point. He didn't understand why it wasn't; he simply knew that Teresa learning that he had once been married wasn't what troubled him. It was the thought of her finding out *like this*. He didn't want her to find out in this way.

Which was mad. Totally crazy. He hadn't planned on telling her anyway. Hadn't thought of telling her *anything*, if he was honest. She was just a one-night stand. Someone with whom he had enjoyed a night of passion, a brief, purely sexual interlude, and nothing more. And if she hadn't woken up before he had left this morning, then she would never have known anything other than that. Never have brought him—and herself—to this uncomfortable moment of revelation.

But that wasn't true either. She hadn't woken by accident. He had deliberately waited for her to wake. He had stayed in the room, sitting in that chair by the window, delaying until she stirred. He could have walked out of the room in any one of a dozen minutes before that, but he hadn't. Something had held him back, kept him there.

And for the life of him he didn't know what.

'Take a look, *cara*,' he drawled now, knowing she must find out and careless of the possible consequences. 'You know you've been dying to, so go right ahead.'

Perversely, now that she had his concession, Terrie found she had lost her nerve, no longer wanting to know what it was that had disturbed him so much. She looked into the darkness of his eyes and felt an icy chill creep through her veins, slowly sliding towards her heart. She was suddenly desperately, bitterly afraid.

'Oh, don't stop now, *belleza*,' Gio goaded her when she hesitated, unable to go any further. 'You fought like a tiger for this—don't turn coward on me now.'

And that 'coward' taunted her into action where nothing else would. Anything less deliberately provocative might have made her hesitate, decide she didn't really want to know, but not this. This deliberate sneer pushed her into doing exactly as he wanted, without even pausing to wonder why he had now decided not to stop her.

But first one tiny, practical part of her mind urged her into protective action, making her take a vital two seconds to pull the tie belt tight about her waist, fasten the robe firmly around her. Only when that was secure did she dare reach for the photographs.

The first one was of a little boy. A beautiful little boy. Quite the most beautiful child Terrie had ever seen. With jet-black hair and deep, dark brown eyes, he was perhaps two years old. He was wearing an oversized T-shirt, white with multicoloured flags on the front, below which just peeped a pair of neat blue shorts. His mouth was stretched in a wide, mischievous grin, and he was clutching a black and white spotted blanket firmly to him.

And Gio didn't have to say a word to explain who the child was, or the man's relationship to him. It was stamped all over the little boy's face, the way it was a perfect, scaled-down replica of Gio's own features.

'Paolo.' Clearly Gio didn't think there was any need of explanation either. 'His name is Paolo.'

'And he's your son.'

He didn't speak to acknowledge her words, which in any case had been a statement, not a question, but his dark head moved in silent agreement anyway.

Which gave her due warning of just what the other photos might show. But all the same it was still a devastating shock, dangerous as a blow to the heart, and potentially as lethal too, as she turned over the next picture and found herself staring into the smiling face of...

'Paolo's mother?' Her voice was just a raw croak as if it had been forced from a desperately sore and infected throat.

'Yes...and my wife.'

CHAPTER SEVEN

TERRIE supposed she should be thankful that at least he had been honest with her, but thankful was the last thing she felt. She wanted to rage at him, to scream and shout, to express her savage feelings in violent language. She was even sorely tempted to launch herself straight at him, hands flying, to pummel angry fists against his hard, unyielding form.

But although the thoughts were there, although the need was like an explosion inside her head, she found that, disturbingly, it was impossible to move. She could only stand there, frozen, her fingers clenched tight on the revealing photograph, her glazed eyes staring unseeingly into the woman's—Gio's *wife's*—face.

What was surprising was that the woman wasn't, in the conventional sense, at all pretty. She was petite and dark, and she had her son's wide, brilliant smile. But no one would ever have called her stunning. She didn't possess a slim, model-like figure either, but was surprisingly rounded at breasts and hips, something that her lack of height accentuated.

'Wha—what's she called?'

And *why* had she asked that? Why did she want to know such a small, but such an intimate detail? Would it make the woman any the more alive, any more *real* if she knew?

How could it? How could anything make this terrible thing more real, more true? If she knew everything about this woman, where and when Gio had met her, how long they'd been married, exactly when the little boy Paolo had been born—when he had been *conceived*—would it make things any easier to bear? Would the pain be any the less because she *knew*—or wouldn't it in fact be impossible to make it any worse?

'Her name is Lucia.'

Why phrase it like that? Gio was forced to wonder. Why not spill out the whole truth and then it would all be out in the open? Why not be strictly accurate, use the correct tense, say 'Her name *was* Lucia'? Because that, after all, was the fact.

But he hated the thought of actually framing the words. Of hearing them spoken out loud like this in this room, in this situation. His clouded gaze went to the wildly ruffled bed where to his astonishment the pillow on the side where he had slept still bore the vague imprint of his head in evidence of the night he had spent there.

OK, so he hadn't been *unfaithful* to Lucia in the strictest sense of the term, but it still felt that way in his heart.

But the problem was that his feelings for Lucia were now further complicated by the present situation.

Porca miseria! He should have gone when he had had the chance!

Or, rather, he should never have acted last night. Never have let his most basic desires, his most primitive needs, cloud his normally cool-headed thinking.

Thinking! The word was like an explosion inside his head. Face it. He hadn't been thinking at all. He had simply been *reacting*. And reacting to the tug of his sexuality, every instinct below the waist, and nothing in his head at all.

And that was what had got him into this mess in the first place.

'Lucia Paolina Cardella.'

'Thank you.'

The ice in her voice stung none the less for being deserved. And the burning glare from those soft-coloured eyes was a bitter reproach to him. Unsettlingly so. Because she had known from the start that it had only been for the night—hadn't she? 'Fun' was what she had said that she was after. She couldn't have expected anything more.

'I'm so glad you finally decided to tell me.'

Her tone said the exact opposite; and the hand that held the photograph tightened convulsively on the picture, threatening to crush it badly.

'*Scusi…*'

Leaning across the bed, he took hold of her hand, trying to lever her clutching fingers free, earning himself another furious glare.

'You are creasing it…'

'So I am!'

For a second she was tempted to rip the photo in two but then, rethinking, decided against it. It wasn't this Lucia's fault that she had an unfaithful rat for a husband. That she was married to a man who couldn't keep his trousers zipped up.

'Here…'

She flung the photograph in Gio's general direction, watching with burning, dry eyes as it flew a little way then floated down to the bed. The way he picked it up, concerned for its appearance, was another cruel twist of the knife in her already desperately wounded heart.

'Don't you think it's rather too late to be concerned?' she questioned bitterly, swallowing down the burning taste of acid in her mouth. 'Last night would have been a better bet if you'd wanted to pretend to have a guilty conscience. Or you could at least have the face to try the old ''my wife doesn't understand me'' routine.'

'It wouldn't be true.'

Gio was looking down at the picture, his concentration intense.

'If you want to know the truth, then Lucia always understood me perfectly.'

'Poor thing…'

The words slipped out before she could catch them back.

'I feel sorry for her. Being married to someone like you. It must be a hell of a life.'

To her horror, her mouth quivered on the last sentence, the words breaking painfully in the middle. And when she looked into Gio's stunning face, saw once again the stony, opaque-eyed look that had settled over his features, it was more than she could do to keep her control. The tears that she had been fighting from the moment that he had headed for the door after telling her he was leaving were now swimming revealingly in her eyes and she set her jaw, swallowing hard, refusing to let them fall.

'Or does she have her—bits on the side as well? Is that it, Gio? Do you have some sort of an open marriage?'

'No!'

The opaque look vanished in an instant. He looked horrified at the thought, shocked right through to the depths of his heart.

No, that was wrong. Not the depths of his *heart*. Giovanni Cardella didn't possess a heart. He couldn't or he wouldn't have behaved in this callous, unfeeling way.

'Lucia would never do any such thing. She has standards…'

That brought her head up sharply, brilliant eyes burning into his in defiance.

'And so do I!'

He had the nerve to look doubtful. Or something. She wasn't at all sure how to interpret the look that flashed across his face, made his gaze suddenly unsteady, but it obviously wasn't total agreement with what she had said.

'I do! I don't sleep with married men, Signor Cardella—at least not when I *know* they are married! But you didn't even have the honesty to tell me! You lied!'

'No...'

'No,' she repeated, her voice dulled by pain. 'No, you never actually lied to me. You just never answered the question, did you? Instead you distracted me with details about your sister-in-law and her pregnancy and the fact that she—she lives in Sicily. With your br-brother. And, I presume—with your *wife*!'

'No.'

'No? Then where...?' Hastily she caught herself up. 'No—don't tell me! I don't want to know! I don't want to know anything about her—or about you—or about your son...'

Liar! her heart reproached her in anguish. Liar, liar, liar!

She *did* want to know—though she would rather have died than to ask him. She wanted to know what had been in his mind when he had approached. Why he had picked on her. Had he truly only wanted a quick sexual fix, a one-night stand, nothing more?

'Teresa...' Gio began.

But the sound of her name on his lips, the wonderful sound of those lyrically accented syllables that had set her heart soaring just a few short hours before, was more than she could bear. It brought her to the edge of her rapidly crumbling control and threatened to push her over.

'Don't say it!' she flung at him. 'Whatever you were

going to say—whatever sort of an excuse you were going to come up with—then don't do it! I told you, I don't want to hear a word! I don't want to know!'

Suddenly too restless with pain to stand still, unable to bear the burn of his watchful ebony eyes, she set up a restless pacing, moving from her side of the bed to the opposite wall of the room in swift, slightly unsteady strides. But there wasn't enough space in the small room to walk as far and as fast as she wanted. Nowhere she could go at the pace that might ease the tearing anguish in her heart, distract her from the bitter burn of the feeling of being used.

'Why did you do it?' she demanded, whirling to face him, blue eyes blazing. 'How could you?'

No, looking into his face had been a mistake. A terrible mistake.

Because just in the second that she had met his eyes once again she had seen something that looked danger-ously, appallingly like—like *compassion*. And that was the last thing that she needed from him. Because it would destroy her. She was barely clinging on to her control as it was.

It couldn't be compassion! She doubted he was capable of feeling any such thing.

'Are you saying you had no part in this?'

Oh, that was better. That was more what she had expected. That was the Giovanni Cardella he had revealed himself to be.

'Of course not!'

She'd be a fool to even try. After all, she'd been the perfect willing victim, just ready and waiting to fall into his greedy, grasping hands like the perfect, ripe plum. She could just imagine how he had felt. As if all his birthdays had come at once. He could never have imagined that she'd be so damn easy that she'd do half the work for him—more than half.

'But at least I never told anything but the truth! I never lied!'

'And neither did I!'

'Oh, no!' Terrie scorned. 'Not half! So you didn't say you *weren't* married—but you dodged the issue quite nicely. And you...you...'

'I what?'

'You called me *cara*! And I told you that that is one Italian word I do understand. *Cara*! You said—'

'I would have said anything at the time. And I'm sure you would too. We all say things we don't mean in the heat of the moment.'

'And if we think it will get us just what we want! Oh—don't look at me like that!' she flung at him when he turned a sidelong glare of reproof on her. 'That's what men do, isn't it? They'll say anything, anything at all if it will get some poor gullible fool into bed with them!'

'I—'

'Oh, don't start backtracking now! Don't try and wriggle out of it! It was all a lie from start to finish. All of it—even—even...'

The knot in her throat threatened to close up completely, making her choke on the words.

'Even when you called me *belleza*.'

'No!'

He shook his head violently in furious rejection.

'No. That was no lie. You are beautiful. Amazing.' He actually sounded as if he meant it. 'You must know that.'

Just for a second Terrie let the words touch her. Let that vehement 'beautiful', that 'amazing' sink in, appease her, soothe the raw wounds he had inflicted on her.

But almost immediately she realised what she was doing, what was happening to her, and pulled herself up sharp.

Was she really going to listen to any more of his lies? Was she going to let him get to her again, reach her, touch her, when she knew that every word he spoke was totally untrue, purely calculated to get what he wanted? Get what he could out of her?

'Oh, no, you don't,' she said, taking a couple of steps backwards, away from him, putting as much distance between them as she could possibly manage in the tiny room.

The movement brought her up against the small table on which the long-cold pot of coffee still stood, the untouched brandy glasses from the previous night.

'You can't think I'd listen to a word you said ever again.'

'Oh, come on!' Gio declared, clearly losing his grip on the temper that had been smouldering dangerously for some time. 'Don't play the outraged virgin in all this! You were as keen for it as I was—more! You brought me up here! You—'

'I what? Threw myself at you? Seduced you?'

'You weren't exactly saying no. And we both knew why you brought me up here. Why you suggested that we have coffee in your room and not in the lounge. "It would be quieter…"' he said suddenly, dropping his voice, softening it, until it was an uncanny and disturbingly accurate copy of her own tones the night before. '"More private". Anyone would have seen what you were up to.'

'So I invited you up for coffee—and you thought that you were in there. That I was yours for the cost of a posh meal and an after-dinner brandy?'

'And you weren't?' he came back at her with the deadly

swiftness of a striking snake as his dark eyes dropped to the tray, resting thoughtfully on the still-full glasses.

'No! No, I wasn't!'

He might have thought she had come cheap, but he couldn't be more wrong. Last night had cost her much, much more than he imagined, and she was only just beginning to realise how expensive it had actually been. But she was damned if she was going to let him see the payment she had made to him in her emotions.

In her heart.

'I'm not that cheap!'

'Forgive me if I beg to differ...'

His tone spoke of anything *but* an apology.

'But neither of us was exactly particular last night. We both saw an opportunity and went for it.'

An opportunity for a quick lay. Terrie didn't know which hurt most. The implication that she hadn't been exactly picky about choosing him. Or the reverse—that if he had had more choice, he might not have wanted to be with her.

But she had been available. Oh, so available. She had been totally bowled over by him and as such had been easy prey for him to take that 'opportunity' he had spoken of.

'Well, in that case...'

Deliberately she kept her voice quiet, calm, hiding the true turmoil of her feelings behind a careful, apparently controlled mask.

'You must be sorry that you didn't have your brandy last night. Something of a waste, don't you think?'

Just as she had planned, hoped, his gaze went to the tray, then back up to her face, a faint frown drawing those straight black brows close together.

And somehow she managed to force a bright, vivid and

totally fake smile right into the darkness of his eyes. One so brilliant that it totally distracted him from just what her hand was doing.

'Perhaps you'd like to have it now?'

The glass was in her grip. She brought it up and out, swiftly, tossing the contents straight into Gio's watchful, puzzled face.

'Enjoy!' she laughed, almost meaning the amusement as she watched him gasp and splutter, wiping the liquid from his face. 'Oh, and while you're at it—you paid for this one too!'

Before he had recovered, the second brandy had followed the first, hitting his chest this time and soaking rapidly into the fine linen of his shirt.

'*Dannazione!*' Gio swore savagely, still wiping the back of his hand across his face, blinking the stinging liquid from his eyes. 'You—'

'Oh, spare me the insults!' Terrie broke in furiously, the pain and the bitterness welling up and overflowing like lava down the sides of a volcano, impossible to stop. 'We both know what you think of me and I don't care to hear it again! We both made a mistake—a big mistake—coming together last night. If I had my time again then believe me I'd have done things totally differently.'

If she'd known what was coming then she'd have run, in the opposite direction, as far and as fast as she could.

'We both would,' Gio inserted drily, uncannily seeming to sense her thoughts.

'Well, we can't put the clock back, it's too late for that. But I'd prefer it if you'd go—right now...'

'Teresa...'

She hadn't expected him to protest and it shook her, weakening her so that the tears she had managed to fight against until now flooded her eyes and threatened to spill over.

'Right *now*!' she flung at him, hiding desperation behind fury. 'I want you to go—get out—leave me in peace.'

Still he hesitated, and she couldn't bear it. She wanted to be left totally alone, to hide and lick her wounds in private. And she was determined that there was no way she was going to break down in front of him.

'Not had enough?' she asked, her voice low and deadly with warning. 'There's always the coffee…'

Her hand had actually reached for the coffee-pot, was curling round the handle, when Gio finally decided to move. Throwing up his hands and muttering something dark and vicious in incomprehensible Italian, he whirled away from her, snatched up his jacket, the wallet and its tumbled contents from the bed, and strode towards the door.

'And don't come back!' Terrie flung at his retreating back.

'You need have no worries on that score,' he tossed right back. 'I'd sooner put my head into the jaws of a hungry lion than ever come up against you again. What is it you say? Good riddance…?'

'To bad rubbish,' Terrie completed for him. 'And believe me, the feeling is totally mutual!'

They were the last words she could manage. The last thing she was capable of saying before weakness totally overwhelmed her and the tears finally started to flow. But she had just enough time. The retort seemed to bounce off the strong, upright line of his back just as he yanked open the door. And he was already out in the corridor by the time that her misery overwhelmed her and she sank down onto the bed.

The sound of the door slamming to behind him was like a sound of release. A signal that at last she was alone. Alone and free to express the volatile combination of anger, betrayal and pain that had been threatening to blow her apart for some time now. Ever since that hateful, that appalling 'and my wife'.

Throwing herself down onto the bed, she pummelled the pillows hard, pounding them in a fury of distress, wishing all the time that they were Giovanni Cardella's hard, lean ribcage. The bones that protected his hard, mean heart.

'I hate you!' she muttered. 'Hate, hate, *hate* you!'

Out in the corridor, Gio didn't even wait for the door to close behind him before he set off at an angry march, heading for the lift. There was just enough room in his buzzing, whirling brain to note, and send up a brief thank-you for, the fact that at this hour of the morning the long, characterless stretches of carpets between the door-lined walls were totally empty. He would have a hard time explaining just what he was doing in such a dishevelled state and reeking of brandy.

Just what *was* he doing?

The question hit home as he punched the call button for the lift, stabbing at it with repressed fury.

How had he managed to make such a complete mess of things?

If he had told Terrie that Lucia was dead, that although he had once been married he was now, in the eyes of society, the church, anyone, a totally free man, then she would not have felt so hurt, so betrayed—so bitterly furious with him.

And she had had every right to feel that way, he admitted to himself as the lift lurched to a halt in front of him and the heavy metal doors slid open. She was completely justified in feeling that hurt, the betrayal, while she thought that he was still married and had simply been playing around, having—what was it the English said? A bit on the side.

But he had *wanted* her to believe that. Preferred her to think that he was an unfaithful husband. That he had deceived both his wife and Teresa, rather than have her know the truth.

And the truth was *what*?

The question was emphasised, underlined in his mind, by the lift doors banging shut again, making him realise that he had been standing still, staring into empty space for who knew how long. Hastily he jabbed one long finger on the call button again, hurrying inside the lift and selecting the penthouse floor before subsiding back into thought once more.

The *truth* was that none of his calculated plans, the coolly thought-up timetable for how things were to go, had actually worked when it had come down to it.

Last night was supposed to have been quick, easy—and above all simple. It was supposed to have been just the swift and temporary sensual indulgence of a one-night stand, no emotions, no commitment involved on either side.

'Madre de Dio!'

Gio raked both hands through the darkness of his hair, noting with a grim touch of amusement that his action did nothing to approve his appearance in the mirror-lined walls of the lift compartment. Instead, he remained as dishevelled-looking as ever, the ruffled hair only adding to the effect of the crumpled, brandy-stained clothes.

He smelled like a drunk, too, he thought, wrinkling his nose in fastidious distaste. Anyone seeing him now would never believe that he and the suave, controlled, articulate counsel for the prosecution in court yesterday were one and the same man.

'Counsel for the prosecution!'

The phrase left his lips on a slightly shaken laugh. He'd certainly been that this morning. He'd condemned *himself* by his silence more effectively than if he'd offered any sort of evidence.

When Terrie had found out that he had a wife, he had deliberately kept back the important detail that Lucia was dead because something had stopped him from speaking. And that something had been that he had wanted her to hate him. Wanted her to throw him out of her room and never have any regrets about her actions afterwards. It would hurt her less that way, he had told himself. She would be able to shake off the memories of the previous night and go on with her life without any afterthoughts.

And he had wanted to ensure that he had no way back. That even if he tried to find his way into her life again, she would slam the door in his face hard and fast.

It had worked perfectly. It couldn't have worked out any better. Terrie had rejected him with all the speed and determination he had expected. He was free. No ties, no commitments.

And he didn't like it.

'Dannazione!' he swore under his breath as the lift came to a halt and the doors rumbled open just by the door to his suite. 'What the hell is wrong with me?'

Wielding his key card like a lethal weapon, he pushed it into the slot and snatched it back out again, wrenching open the door with a force that expressed the disturbed state of his feelings.

What was wrong with him was that he had planned on fixing things so that there was no way back. And now that he'd done just that, he realised it was not what he wanted. Not deep down.

Deep down, what he wanted was more of what he had experienced last night and this morning. He wanted more of Terrie's own special brand of intensely feminine sensuality. More of the deep warmth and passion he had found in her arms. More of the dreamless sleep of satiety that had followed their lovemaking.

And it was a black irony in his mind at the thought that now, finally, he had got exactly what he had set out to achieve last night. Only to find that it was the last thing he truly wanted.

CHAPTER EIGHT

SATURDAY was usually the best day of the week. A day when the prospect of a lie-in, followed by forty-eight hours away from work, gave even the prospect of the most mundane tasks, carried out in the most miserable weather, a glow of anticipation like any other.

But this Saturday was different, Terrie reflected as she pulled on faded denim jeans and a well-worn bright pink T-shirt. Or, rather, it looked set to be almost exactly like every other day this week, and that was what made it a problem.

This time last week, she had had a job. Not the best job in the world, admittedly, but at least it had been *something*. Something that had meant that she was able to support herself, pay the rent on her flat, and maintain a degree of self-esteem.

She no longer had that job. After her absence from two 'vital' elements of the conference her services had been abruptly dispensed with, a decision she hadn't even felt up to arguing about. She had already decided that employment at Addisons had totally lost any of the fragile appeal it had ever held for her. And, as a result of Giovanni Cardella's intervention in her life, self-esteem was something she was totally lacking. He had seen to that, removing all her confidence and leaving her feeling lower than a snail's behind.

'So now what do I do?'

Even the question seemed totally redundant. There was nothing to do.

Free of her job, she had spent the past week cleaning and tidying every inch of her flat. But, as it was basically a living-room-cum-kitchenette plus a single bedroom, with shared bathroom, that hadn't exactly taken long. She had done the basic grocery shopping she could afford, and now the weekend stretched ahead, empty and unappealing.

As a result, the sound of the knock at her door was a more than welcome relief from the prospect, sending her hurrying to respond to it without a second thought as to who might be there. After all, the main entrance into the hall downstairs was always locked, so only someone who shared the house with her could reach the actual door to her flat.

'Is that you, Barbara?'

Expecting to see the woman who lived across from her, the one with whom she shared her bathroom, she was totally unprepared for the tall, dark, dangerously imposing and supremely *male* figure standing on the landing outside.

'*Buon giorno, Teresa,*' drawled a lyrically accented voice that she had thought never, ever to hear again.

'Oh, no, you don't!'

Swift as she was to react, moving instantly to slam the door closed, Gio's responses were even swifter. A large, elegantly booted foot was inserted into the gap between door and frame before she had time to close it properly. A second later a powerful shoulder made contact with the side of the door, wrenching it out of her disturbingly weakened grip, and pushing it wide open once again.

'Good morning, Teresa,' he repeated with a smile that would have melted icebergs. 'It's a pleasure to see you again.'

'And you surely don't expect me to say that the feeling

is in any way mutual,' Terrie flung back, blinking be-musedly in the wake of the brilliance of that smile. 'I thought I told you that I never wanted to see you again? And I meant it!'

'I'm quite sure you did—at the time. But I had hoped that the passage of time would have given you a chance to reconsider and to—'

'Not a hope! I meant what I said and all the reconsid-ering in the world couldn't make me change my mind! I thought I made my feelings perfectly clear last time!'

'And I thought you might like a chance to express them differently— No?' he questioned when he saw the mulish way her jaw set, the stubborn lift to her chin. 'Then it's just as well I came prepared.'

'Prepared?'

Terrie's mouth literally fell open in shocked surprise as Gio lifted the large carrier bag that stood on the floor at his foot, and pushed it into her hands.

'I brought you a gift.'

'A gift—what…?'

In spite of herself she was curious, pulling away the wrapping and revealing what it held inside. An enormous bottle of cognac, the largest she had ever seen, together with a huge balloon-shaped brandy glass made of superb, delicate crystal.

'But…'

'I thought I'd bring you some extra ammunition, just in case you felt you hadn't done enough damage al-ready…'

The wicked smile that tugged at the corners of his mouth, gleaming in the brilliant, dark eyes, was almost irresistible. To her consternation, Terrie actually found herself responding, her own lips curving upwards. Hastily she caught herself just in time, forcing on an expression of stern disapproval that was worryingly hard to maintain.

'After all, those hotel measures are not exactly generous.'

'True,' Terrie was forced to concede.

'And I really felt that you hadn't fully—expressed your feelings last time.'

'True again.'

This was impossible! She wanted to feel anger, hatred, disgust. Wanted to retreat behind the whirlwind of emotion that had assailed her the last time she had seen him. That had been so much safer, a protective shield that protected her from her unwanted feelings for this man. But somehow she couldn't find the same force of reaction that had come to her in her hotel room, much as she longed to.

And she certainly didn't want to feel anything else. But somehow Gio's appearance had sneaked in under her careful defences, aiming straight at a worryingly vulnerable spot in her heart. And he had done it using the unexpected approach of humour, one she hadn't anticipated and so hadn't been able to shield herself against.

'I promise not even to duck.'

His resigned tone, the instinctive squaring of his shoulders was positively the last straw. Terrie fought a swift, hard battle with the amusement bubbling up inside her, trying desperately to force it down—and lost. In spite of herself the laughter she couldn't suppress escaped her on a gasping sigh of defeat.

'Very noble of you, I'm sure. Tell me,' she went on, curiosity getting the better of any sort of sense of self-protection, 'is this supposed to be an apology?'

Gio seemed to consider, dark eyes locking with her interrogative gaze.

'I think I owe you one,' he conceded at last.

Which was so totally unexpected that it actually rocked Terrie back on her heels, depriving her of the ability to speak.

Was this the same Giovanni Cardella she had met in the hotel a week ago? Or had some alien body snatcher taken over his body and replaced him with a very different sort of personality?

'An—an apology for what?' she managed at last when her tongue finally loosened enough to allow her to speak, no longer feeling like a lifeless block of wood in her mouth.

'For not telling you the full truth. Look…'

Gio's tone changed abruptly, the contrition, if that was what it had truly been, vanishing swiftly to be replaced by a note of controlled impatience that was one Terrie recognised much more easily. This was the Gio she knew and recognised only too well.

'Don't you think it would be easier to talk inside? Less public—more private? Anyone might come past here and—'

'You've got a nerve!'

Thankfully Terrie welcomed the rush of irritation, the saving heat of temper that pushed the words from her mouth. Taken aback by the shock of his appearance, the unexpected softness of his words, the nicely calculated humour of his gift, she had come close to a perilous weakness that had left her frighteningly vulnerable to his approaches. She had actually even taken a step backwards, preparing to do just as he suggested, and let him into the flat.

Let him into the privacy of her flat—into the intimate surroundings of her home.

And *privacy* and *intimacy* were two words she didn't

want to consider in connection with Giovanni Cardella. Not if she valued her peace of mind and her emotional safety.

'Turning up here like this—letting yourself into my h… How *did* you get in here?' she demanded when the question she should have asked from the start returned to nag at her brain, this time refusing to be distracted into going away.

'A lady I met at the front door let me in. She said she lived here—flat number two…'

Barbara, Terrie reflected wryly. Of course. It would be. At forty-three and twice divorced, Barbara Roberts was definitely still a sucker for a handsome male face—and she would have been totally unable to resist Gio. If he had turned on the charm—and she had no doubt at all that he *had* done just that—then the older woman would have been putty in his hands from the moment that he had first switched on that wide, bone-melting smile. And if he had treated her to the low-toned, seductive intonation of his wonderful accent, then she would practically have lain down right there on the doorstep and let him walk right over her in order to get what he wanted.

But she wasn't so easily won over, she resolved, pushing aside her momentary weakness of a few minutes before.

'Well, you can just turn right round and walk out again,' she told Gio tartly, mentally promising herself that she would tell Barbara exactly what she thought of her weakness the next time they met. 'I have nothing to say to you—and there is nothing I want to hear—'

'My wife is dead,' Gio broke in on her in a raw-voiced rush. 'Lucia is no longer alive. She died.'

'She…'

For a dreadful moment the room swung around Terrie

sickeningly so that she closed her eyes against the sensation, reaching out and clutching at what she believed was the door for support. But instead of the hardness of wood, her fingers closed over the fine silk of his jacket, clenching over the bone and sinew beneath. And that was every bit as hard as the door, she admitted. Hard, but not cold and unyielding as the wooden panels would have been. She could feel the warmth of his skin, and the flex and play of firm muscle under her grip as he adjusted to her hold, took the full weight of her body and supported it effortlessly.

With a struggle Terrie forced her eyes open again, trying to focus on the hard planes and angles of his stunning face so close to hers, the dark depths of his eyes.

'She's...' she tried again and heard him draw in his breath in a rough-edged hiss between his teeth.

'Dear God, Teresa, no, not that. I did not mean that she had died since that night.'

The rush of relief almost destroyed what little was left of Teresa's already precarious self-control. She hadn't been able to bear even *considering* the possibility that Gio's wife might have died since the night they had spent together in the hotel. Her already uncomfortable conscience couldn't have coped with the thought that they had betrayed the poor woman in the last days of her life.

That *Gio* had betrayed her, she corrected fiercely. He had been the guilty party. The liar, the manipulator, the deceiver.

'Then what did you mean?'

She would have thought that it was impossible for Gio's eyes to grow any darker, for the ebony pools to take her any deeper into his soul. But the shadows that had now surfaced in his gaze clouded their brilliance, dulling it and taking the edge off its clarity.

'I think you should sit down...'

His tone held nothing but concern, almost shocking in its unexpected gentleness, as he guided her carefully towards a chair.

Too late, she realised what he had done; how he had manipulated her yet again. The slam of the door closing behind him told its own tale—of how Gio had seized his opportunity, taking advantage of the way that she was totally distracted, knocked off balance by his shocking statement. He had ignored her obvious determination not to let him into her flat, and had moved forward, coming into the room on the pretext of taking care of her, gaining his own objective without any trouble.

'I don't want to sit down. And I think that *you* should explain!'

He was making a real mess of this, Gio reflected grimly. He had never meant to blurt out the truth about Lucia in quite that way, but when it had come to the point there had been no other way. He wanted Terrie to know the truth, but actually saying the words 'My wife is dead' was still so difficult, so painful, that his throat had almost closed over the words, blocking them off. In the end he had had either to force them out, rough and devastatingly blunt as they were, or play the coward and leave them unsaid once more.

And he had vowed to himself that he would never do that.

'I'll explain,' he growled roughly. 'Just tell me what you want to know.'

'I want to know everything...'

As she spoke she twisted away from his grasp and he didn't know whether he was glad to let her go or if what he really wanted was to hold her tighter, pull her closer to him, feel her warmth and the scent of her skin enclose him once more. The loss of the physical contact felt as though something vital had been ripped away from him, and yet at the same time it was a relief to be freed from the temptation that her body offered.

For the past week without her he had been trying to convince himself that it had all been a delusion. That the night he had spent with her had been a fleeting sexual pleasure, nothing more. He had told himself that no woman could have had such an effect on him, that he couldn't have been so instantly smitten by her. That he was exaggerating the concentrated, mind-blowing effect she had had on him.

It was only his hunger remembering, he had told himself. The hunger that was the result of two years' abstinence, two years' celibacy since he had lost Lucia. She couldn't have been so devastating. So unforgettable. So irresistible.

But now that he was here with her, he knew that by denying the effect she had on him he had been deceiving himself. She was everything he remembered—and more. When she had opened the door to him, just the sight of her had had an effect like a blow in his face, making his thoughts reel in instant response. His body had tightened, hardened, clamoured in protest at the restraint he had had to impose on himself. And now, being in the same room with her and not touching her, not kissing her...and more was a physical torment that made his yearning senses scream in agonising demand.

But he had to keep his distance. Had to hold himself together and not give in to hunger that was like an ache in every cell. At least until he had told her the truth.

'So where do you want me to begin?'

The withering glare she turned on him from those beautiful eyes might have quelled a lesser man. As it was, he felt the ice in it seem to penetrate his flesh, chilling, if only for a second, the heated rush of his blood.

'They say that the beginning is a good place to start.'

The beginning. The beginning was when he and Lucia had been so young, so innocent. Little more than children when they had first met. Barely in their teens when they had known that they were right for each other—meant to be together. But those were his memories, and his alone. She had no right to any part of them.

'Gio…'

Terrie's tone warned that he had hesitated too long.

'Either tell me or…'

She didn't have to finish the sentence. The swift flicker of her eyes towards the door, the stubborn set of her jaw, the defiance in her gaze, all made her meaning more than plain. Drawing in his breath on a rough, uneven hiss, Gio raked one hand forcefully through his hair.

'Lucia and I were married for over ten years…'

'Ten!' She hadn't expected that. 'You must have been…'

'Childhood sweethearts.'

Gio's confirmation was grim.

'She was all I had ever wanted in a woman—in a wife. I loved her from the start—and I never stopped loving her.'

His tone defied her to question the stark assurance of the declaration. But Terrie had no thought of doing any such thing.

He had *loved* his wife. She could have no doubt about that. It was there in the clouded depths of his eyes, the tautness of his jaw, the raw, roughened note in his words.

And it brought both a glorious excitement to her mind and in the same instant a terrible chill to her heart to see it there and recognise it for what it was.

What Gio had felt for Lucia had been true love. Total love. The sort of love that she had only ever dreamed a man could feel. The sort of love that she had prayed she might one day find for herself, if she was truly lucky.

But Gio hadn't felt that love for her. His heart had been given to another woman long ago, and she was beginning to doubt if there was anything left in it for anyone else.

'What happened?'

'We were married. We planned on the whole happy-ever-after—home, kids, everything. For a while we had everything, even the baby she dreamed of.'

'Paolo.'

'Yes, Paolo.'

Something changed in Gio's expression, his jaw clenching, his gaze losing focus. On an abrupt movement he swung away from her, pacing across the room to stand and stare out of the window, hands pushed deep into the pockets of his expensively tailored jacket. He assumed an intense interest in the traffic going past in the street, but Terrie had caught the betraying sheen filming his eyes, and the stiff, defensive set of those broad shoulders told its own story.

The need to touch him, to try to reach him, to communicate her understanding was almost overwhelming, but a terrible sense of uncertainty held her back. If she went to him now he might reject her, repulse her tentative gesture with an angry impatience or worse. And, feeling as she did right now, she knew she couldn't bear that.

Since the moment that he had appeared at her door again, her emotions had been on a roller-coaster ride of reaction. Shooting up in the simple delight of seeing him one moment, only to plunge down into the depths of despair at the knowledge of how little she meant to him the next.

She wanted to hate him. Hate him for the way he had treated her. The way he had used her and discarded her without a second thought. Hate was simple and easy and it precluded all other, more dangerous emotions. But hatred wasn't what she felt for him. She'd tried and, in spite of everything, had found that that wasn't what was in her heart.

And that was the truly scary thing.

'So you had Paolo…'

She had to force herself to speak. The broad, unyielding wall of his back couldn't have been any more off-putting if it had had notices pinned to it. *Go away! Keep out! Trespassers will most definitely be prosecuted.* The words didn't have to be spoken. They hung in the air like a deep grey cloud all around him.

'Was there a problem?'

'No.'

Gio's voice sounded as if it came from a long, long way away.

'No problem. The birth was fine. The baby was fine. Lucia…was fine. Or so everyone thought. We brought the baby home…'

Without warning he swung round, and, having hoped that he would no longer turn his back on her, Terrie now desperately wished the opposite. His face was almost unbearable to see. It seemed impossible that the deep lines of pain and distress etched around his nose and mouth, the bruised shadows in his eyes, could have appeared in such a short space of time.

'What happened?'

'Ten days before Paolo's first birthday, Lucia was alone in the kitchen and she collapsed. Suddenly and unexpectedly—there had been no sign of anything wrong. She'd complained of a faint headache, but that was all.'

He drew in a long, rawly rasping breath before he could go on.

'She died that night. There was nothing they could do for her. A brain haemorrhage, the doctors said. Something that could never have been predicted.'

'Oh…'

It was all that Terrie was capable of managing. She wanted to hold him. To weep for him. To do anything that she thought might help. But at the same time she didn't dare.

Her hands went to her face, covering her eyes for a second, then her mouth. Then she half extended them towards him, but almost immediately rethought and pulled them back. As long as she didn't know how Gio was going to react, she wasn't going to open herself to an attack or a rejection that would destroy her. She couldn't take any more of that.

'And every day since then I've never gone to sleep without wishing that I could tell her how much I loved her just one more time.'

'I'm—'

'No!' he cut in savagely, eyes blazing dangerously. 'Don't say you're sorry! I never want to hear that word again, at least not in this context. I had a bellyful of "sorry"s in the months after it happened—after Lucia died. Everyone I met said they were sorry—how sorry they were…'

'They were only trying to help.'

'Maybe they were—but it doesn't help. Nothing helps at a time like that. What makes them think that "sorry" will somehow put it right?'

'I don't know,' Terrie admitted. 'I've never been through a loss like that.'

Somehow her words got through to him. She saw his

head go back, a tiny hint of the tension leaving his long body, a calmer light coming into his eyes.

'Well, that's honest at least. You wouldn't believe how many people will say that they know how you feel.'

'I couldn't begin to *imagine* how you feel. I wouldn't even try.'

It would hurt too much, even to feel it *for* him, never mind to have to go through it herself.

She wished there was something—anything she could do that would help. But all that her numbed, bruised mind could come up with was the simple, practical matters that would ease the here and now, because they could do nothing about the past.

'You look as if you could do with a drink. Why don't you sit down while I get you something?'

'Do you mean to say that I get to drink the brandy this time?'

As an attempt at humour it was weak and disturbingly shaky, twisting in Terrie's vulnerable heart. And the obvious effort that it had cost him to say it spoke much more of the way he was feeling than any outpouring of words could ever do, so that she struggled to raise even the faintest glimmer of the smile that she felt he had been aiming for.

'Perhaps it's a little early for the hard stuff. How about a coffee? I've only instant, I'm afraid.'

'Coffee would be fine—instant—anything.'

Did he know how grateful she was for the excuse to get away from him, escape into the kitchen just for a minute? Terrie wondered. Would he realise how much she needed to gather herself, collect her scattered thoughts, recoup her shattered defences? Or would he just think she was so totally switched off from him that she didn't care one way or another and she was simply going through the motions, using politeness and courtesy to cover a difficult situation?

Quite frankly, right now, she didn't care! She no longer even felt like the same person who had opened the door to find Gio standing outside at the start of the morning. She just needed a little time…time to focus on the tiny practical matters that seemed like such a refuge from the storm of emotions that assailed her. Concentrating fiercely, as if what she was doing was a matter of life and death, she filled the kettle, switched it on, collected mugs…

She was reaching for the coffee from the cupboard when Gio spoke behind her unexpectedly.

'I take it black.'

With an effort, Terrie managed not to drop the coffee jar as she nodded, grateful for the fact that he couldn't see her face, or the shock of reaction that must be her expression, giving away far more than was truly safe.

'OK. That's probably just as well. To tell the truth, I'm not exactly sure about the milk situation. I haven't bought any fresh for a couple of days.'

She was talking to fill the silence, she knew. Saying something, anything, that might distract her from the fact that he was there, just behind her, so close she could almost hear the soft sound of his breathing, feel the heat of his body reach out to enclose her.

'Sugar?'

'No, thanks.'

She had no choice but to turn now. No choice but to face him. Not unless she was going to stand here forever, looking like a total idiot, frozen in mid-action, unable to decide whether to move or not.

'Good. I'm not sure whether I have any of that either.'

She'd whirled round as quickly as she could, taken the

few steps across the room to the kettle, desperately trying to avoid looking at him, but it was no use. The kitchen was tiny enough on an ordinary day, and today, with Gio's tall, dark, lethally sexy presence filling it, it seemed to have shrunk to mouse-hole proportions.

'Why don't you ask me, Teresa?'

'Ask you what? I—I don't have…'

His arrogantly impatient flick of his hand, the way his tongue clicked against his teeth dismissed her protest as the prevarication that it was.

'You know perfectly well what I mean. The problem that's been nagging at you ever since you opened the door to me. The question you've been dying to ask…'

'I have?'

His dark head moved in a nod of agreement. And although deep inside she knew just what he meant, she also knew that she couldn't bring herself to say it. Couldn't just blurt it out in a rush, without hesitation, straight into his face. Her throat would close up against the words if she even tried.

'You want to know why I'm here. What I want of you. So why don't you just go ahead and ask me?'

CHAPTER NINE

'I KNOW why you came.'

Terrie knew she was dodging the issue and she suspected that Gio realised it too. Once again there had been another of those subtle shifts in the atmosphere in the room; a tightening of the pressure up a couple of notches. And because of the confined space in the microscopic kitchen it felt as if the tension had permeated the actual air around them so that it was thick and heavy, making it difficult to breathe.

'You came to apologise.'

Dumping coffee granules into a mug, she slopped on boiling water and stirred it with unnecessary ferocity.

'At least that's what you said.'

He had also said, 'You want to know why I'm here. What I want of you.' But she wasn't going to go down that road. It was too dangerous, totally uncharted territory. She had no idea what threats, what risks lay hidden along it.

'But you haven't exactly *apologised*, have you?'

She couldn't stir the coffee any longer without looking a complete fool. She must be close to scraping a hole in the bottom of the mug as it was.

Turning, she pushed the mug at Gio, heedless of the way that some of the hot liquid spilled over the side and onto the floor.

'*Have* you?'

'I said I regretted not having told you the whole truth.'

He took the mug she held out, his long fingers brushing

against hers as he did so, making her want to flinch and start backwards as if she had brushed against an exposed live electrical wire, burning her skin.

'What else did you want?'

There was a definite challenge in the dark eyes now, almost, but not quite driving away the deep shadows of just moments before. Had he truly recovered so bewilderingly fast? Or was he just dangerously skilled at hiding his true feelings behind a careful, emotionless mask? The answer to that question was one that Terrie was not at all sure she wanted to know.

'I...'

'I'm not going to apologise for something we both consented to.'

Eyes the colour of the rich coffee in his mug seared over her face, probing like a dark laser under the black brows that drew together sharply in an ominous frown.

'Or are you going to try and claim that I forced you?'

'Oh, no!'

She wouldn't dare! She *couldn't*. It was impossible even to think of it when she knew that denying his claim would be the worst lie she had ever told.

'No. I'm not saying that.'

'*Bene.*'

His nod was curt to the point of dismissive.

'Because I feel no guilt for something we both wanted...'

Dark eyes skimmed over her again, lingering appreciatively on her mouth, her throat, the swell of her breasts as they rose and fell with her uneven, nervous breathing.

'Something we'd both like to do again.'

But that was too much.

'Something *you* might like to do again!' Terrie protested. 'I don't remember having said any such thing.'

'Not *said*,' was Gio's drawling agreement. 'But then sometimes there is no need for anyone to say anything. The signs are there, clear to read. In the glance of an eye, a smile…'

Slowly he leaned forward and trailed the back of his free hand softly down her cheek and under her jaw.

'In a glow you can't hide…'

The pad of his thumb smoothed across the fullness of her lips, awakening a deep inner hunger just with the single caress.

'A softness of the mouth…'

'Don't!'

With a fierce movement that was totally unnecessary, considering the gentleness of his hold, she wrenched her head away from his grasp. The struggle to ignore the fizzing sensation along every nerve made her voice hard and tight as she rounded on him.

'You're reading the signs all wrong if that's what you think!'

It was almost impossible to hear the words through the wild pounding of her heart.

'Or perhaps you're simply finding what you want to see, because I'll tell you that your sordid fantasies are just not true!'

'Is that a fact?'

Gio's slow, faintly mocking smile almost undid her totally, sending shivers of reaction running down her spine, though for the life of her she couldn't decide whether they were of fear or tingling excitement.

'Well, you can protest all you like, *carina*, but just remember that I am the one who can see your face, look into your eyes… And I assure you that there is nothing *sordid* about my fantasies—nothing at all!'

'I—' Terrie began, but he swept on, ignoring the fact that she had even tried to speak.

'They are simply that I wish to repeat the pleasures of our night together, over and over again. And I know that you do not consider those pleasures in any way sordid. How could you, when you were the one who instigated most of them—and who actively encouraged the ones I contributed?'

Expertly manoeuvred into a corner, mentally if not physically, Terrie admitted to cowardice and didn't even try to respond, resorting only to turning a fulminating glare on his wickedly smiling face, a scornful, but inarticulate, 'Huh!' the only sound that escaped her.

But inside her mind was buzzing, replaying unwanted memories, projecting dangerously erotic scenes from their night together onto the screen of her thoughts. Just that brush of his thumb across her mouth had reminded her of the taste of his skin, the scent of his hand, the way that his touch made her feel. She felt unnervingly on edge, frighteningly restless and close to veering out of control.

All the secret, intimate places on her body seemed to wake, clamouring for more of that touch. Her mouth hungered to know again the deeply personal taste of his flesh. And the reason for all those feelings was right there beside her, his height and strength dominating the small space of her kitchen, making her feel as if it had suddenly shrunk to a quarter of its size.

Swallowing hard, she forced herself to speak with a degree of control that she was far from feeling.

'I think we'd both be more comfortable if we went through into the living room and sat down.'

Her voice was cool and tight, obviously intended to be quelling. But Gio knew that it would take more than a few words to crush down the heavy throb of desire that his whole body was a prey to.

Comfortable! he reflected on a twist of cynicism. Feeling *comfortable* was the last thing possible when he was so close to this woman. In fact, he doubted whether even moving into the other room and sitting further away from her would help. Every cell in his body was on red alert to the sight, the sound, the scent of her.

And touching her had been a mistake.

A *bad* mistake!

As soon as his thumb had brushed across her mouth, her lips had softened under his touch, reminding him of how it had felt to take them in the heat of a passionate kiss. His skin had touched the warm, moist interior, reminding him of the heated slickness of the feminine warmth that had closed around him countless times during their night together, and the urge to grab her, haul her hard up against him and kiss her senseless had almost got the better of him.

Almost. But at the last moment what little sanity he had left had prevailed—thankfully!

Grabbing Teresa Hayden was quite the wrong way to go about things, at least this time. Last time he had grabbed—and so had she—and they had both ended up in a situation that was quite out of their control. They had been caught up in a maelstrom of passion that had obliterated any hope of sensible thought, whirling them up out of the rational world and into a fierce, blazing inferno of need that would allow for no resistance.

And tonight he had promised himself that he would think—or at least try to think—with what was inside his head, not what was below his belt, and he was damned well going to stick to that resolve if it killed him. Which was what it looked likely to do if he didn't pull back and put some distance between the two of them—fast!

'After you...'

Even as he spoke the words he felt the sense of shock at his own stupid mistake. To allow her to go first meant that he would have to let her squeeze past him in the confined space of the doorway, coming closer than ever before.

The soft brush of her pert buttocks against his already hardened groin was a source of delicious agony that had him biting down hard on his lower lip so as not to groan aloud in uncontrollable response. Her silky blonde hair wafted against his face, the scent of it combining with the intimate, deeply personal aroma of her skin tormenting his hotly aroused body with its sensual caress. And he had to clench his fingers hard on the handle of his coffee mug so that the tremor in his grip didn't betray him by spilling some of the liquid onto the floor.

Dio—sucurro! he thought on a wave of despair, closing his eyes and letting his head fall back against the hard wood of the doorjamb. How had he ever let this woman reduce him to such a state of sexual slavery so fast? How had she brought him to this point where every movement she made, every glance from those lavender-coloured eyes, every sound of her voice was pure intoxication, total seduction?

'Gio?'

Terrie was clearly puzzled by the fact that he hadn't moved.

'Are you coming?'

Oh, yes...

Hastily he caught himself up, shaking his dark head hard, blinking as he forced away the last clinging strands of the erotic daydream that had had him in its grip.

'*Sì,*' he said in a very different tone, the crisp, cool note totally erasing the husky fervency of his thoughts of just moments before. 'Yes, of course I am.'

He might move into the room, but he couldn't sit down. He felt restless, edgy, a cat on hot bricks. And unknowingly Terrie only made matters worse by the way she curled up in her chair, depositing her coffee mug on the tiled hearth to her left before turning to face him.

She looked like an innocent young girl with her legs tucked up under her like that, the blonde hair tumbling about her face, falling onto the slender shoulders in the bright pink T-shirt. But the body outlined by the clinging soft cotton was all woman, the thrust of her breasts proclaiming her femininity for anyone to see. The position of her legs meant that the worn, faded denim had tightened around the sweet curves of her hips and buttocks, clinging to the length of her thighs, adding to the sensual provocation that had tormented him only moments before.

'So why did you come here today?'

And how did he answer that? Gio took a swallow of his coffee to ease a suddenly dry throat, and grab at some last-minute thinking time, then set his mug down on the mantelpiece as he turned to her.

To hell with thinking. He would just tell her the truth.

'I came because I couldn't stay away.'

'Oh, sure!'

The look she turned on him was frankly sceptical, darkening the soft eyes to a deep, opaque grey.

'Sure! I'll be honest with you—'

'I wish you would.'

'I will! I'll tell you the truth if you'll only shut up and listen for once! Do you ever let anyone speak without arguing?'

'As a matter of fact I do—most of the time,' Terrie

returned stiffly. 'It's just that you seem to have this bad effect on me.'

'And you on me,' Gio retorted. 'But all the same, this time I am telling the truth—the whole truth...'

And nothing but the truth. The words echoed ominously inside Terrie's head, giving her the unwelcome reminder that the man before her was a renowned international lawyer, at the very top of the ladder. It seemed that ever since she had met him in the hotel last week the papers had been full of accounts of his skills, his prowess in the courts. She couldn't imagine how she had ever come to miss him before.

'Go on,' she managed stiffly, the thought suddenly draining all the fight from her so that she slumped down in her seat, not daring to look him straight in the eye.

'As I said, I came here today because I couldn't stay away. Last week, I thought I could. I thought that was what I wanted. I thought that was what you wanted too.'

'What was what I wanted?'

'A one-night stand. Some fun—nothing more.'

'Fun!'

The single syllable was a strangled sound in Terrie's throat.

'You thought...'

Hastily she swallowed down the rest of her retort, knowing that to say what she really thought could only make matters so much worse.

'Go on,' she said stiffly.

Gio was pacing around the room, hands pushed deep into the pockets of his trousers, his restlessness as unnerving as having a tiger caged up with her, watching its hungry prowling.

'I thought I could walk away and forget about you, but

it didn't work out that way. I couldn't get you out of my mind.'

For the first time Terrie actually sat up a little straighter, her interest piqued. She had been sure that what he was going to say was simply another put-down, something that would make her feel worse than ever. Now, at last, there was a tiny spark of hope that perhaps it could be different.

'I couldn't stop thinking about you. I couldn't eat; I couldn't sleep. I couldn't concentrate on my work.'

And his tone said that *that* was unusual. That in the past his work had always been able to hold him.

'I had to see you again. I couldn't leave without seeing you once more...'

'Leave!'

There was that word again, but this time it sounded different.

'You're going away?'

Her sudden interjection had stopped his restless pacing, brought him swinging round to face her.

'I'm flying out tomorrow.'

'But where...?'

'I'm going back home—to Sicily.'

'*I'm going...*' Terrie noted; not 'I was going' or 'thinking of going.'

Which was worse? she couldn't help asking herself. If he had left without saying a word, without ever coming back, so that she had never, ever seen him again? Or the fact that he was here now, giving her foolish, vulnerable heart the chance to think, to dream for a moment? The opportunity to allow it to form the impossible fantasy that he might want more than he had said that first night? That there might be the tiniest possibility of a future, however brief, for them together?

And as soon as she had allowed the thought into her

mind she knew, on a painful clench of her heart, just how much that hope had come to mean to her.

'So this is goodbye?'

'It doesn't have to be.'

'But that's what you came to say? That you were leaving.'

'Teresa...'

Gio pulled both strong hands from his pockets and raked them through the dark sleekness of his hair in a gesture that revealed the ruthless control he was struggling to impose on himself.

'I *have* to go. I have to be there. It's my son's third birthday on Tuesday. I promised him I'd be home for that.'

Of course. Paolo.

'Who's looking after him now?'

She asked the inconsequential question simply in order to say something. Anything, to fill the silence that had descended as soon as Gio had stopped speaking. Because the truth was that she had no idea what else to say. There was nothing she *could* say. Gio had made up his mind. His plans were fixed, and he was determined to go and there was nothing she could say to stop him.

And did she want to stop him? The sudden rush of anguish that wrenched at her heart at the thought of watching Gio turn his back and walk out on her once more, for good this time, told her the answer to that. But it was an answer that solved no problems. Instead it only seemed to make matters immeasurably worse.

'...in Taormina,' Gio finished and to her horror she realised she hadn't heard a word of what else he had said.

'I'm sorry...' she stumbled, past caring how foolish it made her look. 'Who lives in Taormina?'

'Paolo's grandparents.'

His searching, probing glance made it plain that he wanted to know the reason for her distraction, her lack of concentration, but to Terrie's relief he didn't question her about it but answered her question equally enough.

'My mother and stepfather. And sometimes he spends time with Cesare and Megan.'

'Oh, yes, Megan—your sister-in-law.'

Terrie flinched inwardly as the name reminded her of the conversation she had had with Gio on that first night in the hotel. Just before he had turned to her and held out his hand.

'Come here to me, *belleza*,' he had said. 'Come here… and let's finish what we've started.'

'S-so Cesare is your brother?'

She spoke hastily in an effort to erase the painful memories, to crush down the bitter acid that was rising in her throat.

'Half-brother. My father died before I was a year old and my mother married again. Cesare is her son with her second husband, Roberto Santorino.'

'And how long have you been away—from Paolo?'

'Three weeks.'

Gio's quick frown told her that this wasn't the sort of conversation he wanted to be having, the topic he had planned to discuss, but she didn't care. Each ordinary word that she spoke, each matter-of-fact statement or question, seemed like another brick inserted carefully into the wall with which she hoped to surround herself. The barriers that would serve as her defence against the moment when he said that he was leaving—and that he wasn't coming back.

'He'll have missed you.'

'He'll be glad to see me again.' Gio nodded. 'I've talked to him every night on the phone, but it just isn't the same. There's no substitute for being able to hold someone in your arms.'

'No...'

It was as much as she could manage and she had to gulp the words down in the same moment as she fiercely swallowed the tears she wouldn't let fall. *Couldn't* let flow in spite of the way they burned in her eyes, forcing her to blink back the stinging liquid. If she had so much as a phone call to look forward to from Gio, then it would be something, but this time with him, such as it was, was all there would be. Once he was back in Sicily, he wouldn't contact her again. Probably wouldn't even spare her a thought, in spite of all his protestations that he hadn't been able to get her out of his mind. Once he was home, and back with his family, he would forget all about her.

While she would have nothing but memories. Memories that, if this past week was anything to go by, would come back to haunt her in the darkness of the night, in the silence and the stillness, when she was at her lowest possible ebb and totally incapable of holding them back.

'He—he must be counting the hours.'

'He's also looking forward to seeing my new friend.'

'He—he *what*?'

The sudden realisation of just what he had said had her sitting forward, blue-grey eyes locking with deepest brown.

'My son is looking forward to meeting my new friend,' Gio repeated, coolly and clearly and elaborately slowly. 'He wants to see you.'

'I don't understand.'

She was leaning forward as she spoke, reaching for the coffee mug on the hearth, needing something to do—anything—to distract her from the look in his eyes, the buzzing confusion in her head.

'It's quite straightforward, Teresa. I am returning to Sicily. I have to go back for Paolo—and I want you to come with me.'

'You...'

Hastily Terrie put her half-raised mug back down onto the tiles before she let it fall completely. She felt as if his words had caused her heart to stop abruptly then jolt back into action with an uneven judder.

Had he really said what she believed he had?

'I'm flying back to Sicily tonight. I want you to come with me.'

Even when he had said the actual words, Terrie still couldn't quite bring herself to believe them.

'Why?' she croaked.

Gio's sigh was a perfectly calculated blend of resignation and exasperation.

'Teresa, *cara*, we have been through this before. I told you—'

'I know what you told me but I don't believe it!'

Didn't dare believe it. Couldn't let the possibility that his outrageous claims might be the truth into her head because if she did then she was only opening herself to a more devastating hurt than before because she had allowed herself to hope.

'Believe it!'

Gio's voice was harsh, deep, vibrating with the emphasis on the words as he came to stand in front of her, placing one hand on each arm of the chair and leaning over her to stare deep into her face.

'Believe it, *belleza*, because it is the truth! I want you to come to Sicily with me, because this last week I have thought I am going crazy without you. Because I spend my days thinking of you when I should be working.'

'You do?'

'All the time,' he assured her.

Terrie gazed up into his dark, set face, unable to think beyond the small excited voice that was repeating over and over in her head, He wants me with him! He wants me with him! And, seeing the bemused, still not totally convinced expression on her face, Gio held out a hand to her. Like a hypnotist's mindless victim, she put her own fingers into it and let his strength draw her upwards, out of her seat, until she was standing so close to him that she felt her body melting into the heat of his.

'I want you with me because at night I dream of holding you close...'

He suited the action to the words, drawing her into the circle of his embrace, folding his arms around her.

'Of running my hands through your hair...kissing your soft mouth.'

Long fingers fastened in her hair, bringing her face to his, and his lips closed over hers in a long, demanding kiss that made her senses swim wildly. On a tiny murmur of surrender, she abandoned all pretence at keeping her distance and gave herself up to the seductive spell he was weaving around her. Her hands went up and around his neck, her mouth softening, opening under his.

Her body was curved against the lean, hard length of him, the wild demand of sexual hunger uncoiling low down in her body in the space of a heartbeat. And when one of those exploring hands left her hair and slid down her spine, closing over her hip to press her even closer into contact with the potent force of his erection, she caught in her breath on a swift, choking sigh of mindless yearning.

His kiss was stealing away her soul, taking with it all hope of thinking rationally, of being able to reason in any way at all. She could only respond, only surrender to the forceful, primitive tug of sexual attraction that would always bind this man and her together.

'I can't sleep for thoughts of kissing you…touching you, possessing you,' Gio murmured against her mouth. 'My whole body aches with wanting you. I couldn't leave without seeing you again. That's why I came here today—to ask you to come home with me.'

Come home. The words had such a wonderful sound. They seemed to hold the very essence of her dreams, the core of the unspoken hopes that had shimmered in her mind on the night they had met. They whispered of togetherness and sharing, of the possibility of a future.

He wanted her to go home with him. To meet his child. His family. Her heart clenched on a pleasure that was sharp as a pain. Her mind was just a red-gold haze, blurring under the assault, both physical and mental, on all her senses.

'So, what do you say, *cara*?' Gio whispered, his lips against her hair. 'What's your answer? Will you come? Will you—?'

'Yes!'

She couldn't wait for him to finish. Didn't need him to complete the question when already she knew in her heart that she had decided and that there was no going back. The long, lonely hours of the past week, the tears she had shed in the darkness of the night, had taught her one thing.

If there was a chance, even the tiniest hope, that they could start again then she would reach out with both hands and grab it, holding on tight.

'Yes!' she said again, even more emphatically than before. 'Yes, I'll come with you. I'd love to! I can't wait! It won't take me a minute to pack and—'

'And what about your job?' Gio inserted the question

into the excited flow of her response, the ardent lover suddenly submerged beneath cool practicality.

His abrupt change of mood was rather disconcerting, the sudden stillness of his powerful body, the sharp scrutiny in his eyes bringing a sensation like the slow scraping of sandpaper over uneasily raw nerves.

'My job? Oh, that doesn't matter!'

Why did it have to happen now? Gio wondered. Why, when it was the last thing he wanted, did he have to remember moments from that evening they had spent together? Moments that hinted at another side to Terrie, a colder, more grasping side than the warm and willing woman he held in his arms.

'I can't expect fairy godfathers to come along every day of the week, can I?' she had said, and he had wondered whether she had hoped to cast him in the role of that 'fairy godfather' long-term.

'You said you planned on "chucking" it.'

'If you want the truth then no, I don't have a job any more. Not that I got a chance to chuck it. My employment at Addisons only lasted long enough for me to be interviewed by the boss on Monday and decide that it would be mutually beneficial if I left at once. In fact, if you'd not turned up here tonight you might not have found me. I was already beginning to wonder how I could afford to keep this place on, and I would probably have rung my parents and asked if I could come home.'

Instead of which, he had turned up just in time.

For a second, Gio was tempted to revoke his invitation. To say that he had made a mistake, changed his mind. He no longer wanted her to come to Sicily with him.

But that would be nothing but a lie. And a total denial of the way he was feeling. The needs he had been fighting against all week, only to know that he could hold out no longer. To admit that he could not just turn his back and walk away as he had once planned. That he had to have her once more or he would go insane with wanting.

He had told her the truth about the hunger, the emptiness he had felt all week. But until he had heard the words come out of his mouth, he had never known that he had even thought of inviting her to come back to Sicily with him. But perhaps now that he had said it, it would be the best way to work things. This way he could both have his cake and eat it, as the English saying went.

And it would serve one other, vitally important function too. It would solve another concern that had been nagging at him since his uncharacteristic loss of any sort of sense—except one—during the night they had spent together.

'Then you'll welcome a chance for four weeks in the sun?'

There it was again, that disturbingly controlled edge to his voice, Terrie recognised on a shiver of apprehension. And if she had been asked to define the look in his eyes then 'calculating' would have been the word that came to mind. The passionate, seductive Gio had evaporated like mist before the sun, and in his place was a cold-eyed analyst. A man who made her feel uncomfortably like some carefully prepared specimen on a laboratory slab, ready for dissection.

'Four weeks?'

Foolishly, she hadn't thought in terms of a set span of time. She knew that Gio wasn't promising a lifetime's commitment, but she hadn't quite expected that their time together would be so clearly defined.

'Why four weeks?'

'I think that should be long enough to be sure.'

Sure? This time she swallowed the question down,

afraid to voice it. A few moments ago she might have been naïve enough to think that Gio was talking about being sure of the way he felt about her, but now the sudden change in his demeanour, the subtle shift in his whole attitude to her was setting off warning bells inside her brain. Suddenly disturbingly ill at ease, she stiffened in Gio's embrace, holding her body away from him.

'Don't you think?'

It was asked with such total calm, such a complete lack of any emotion that it made her blood run cold just to hear it.

'And what precisely do you need to be sure about?'

'Don't play the fool, Teresa!' Gio's tone was a chilling mixture of cynical amusement and curt dismissal. 'You're not a complete innocent, so don't pretend that you are. You know what happened that night we spent together. We didn't take any precautions—at any time. You know—precisely—what might have happened. What the result of our affair might be.'

If Terrie's blood had chilled a few moments before, now it felt as if it was turning to ice in her veins. And the cold seemed to have reached her brain, destroying any chance of thinking clearly enough to answer Gio in this form—once more Giovanni Cardella, counsel for the prosecution.

'Nothing happened!' she flung at him in a nervous rush, twisting against his loosened hold and freeing herself with a jolt that took her partway across the room away from him. 'Don't honour what we had with the title of an affair—it was nothing like! It was a sordid little one-night stand in a hotel bedroom after you picked me up in a bar, nothing more! And there won't be any result!'

'And you can swear to that, can you? Am I to take it that—?'

'No!'

Even to outface him, she found she couldn't lie to him about this. But all the same she couldn't stop herself from taking several nervous backward steps, away from him. He was too big, too dangerous-looking to have towering over her like this.

'If you're trying to ask if I've had a period since last Saturday, then the answer's no—no, I haven't! But it's nothing for you to worry about! It'll be fine! I know it will!'

'So you were on the Pill?'

He read the answer in her face before she managed to find the words to say it and his beautiful mouth twisted cynically.

'No...' he said grimly. 'No Pill—no protection of any sort. And you still think you won't be pregnant.'

Pregnant. The word seemed to hang in the air between them like an insurmountable barrier that had to be dealt with, got out of the way, before anything else could be said or even considered.

'I'll be fine...'

Terrie knew she was stumbling over the words, struggling to dodge the issue that had been preying on her mind all week. Time and time again she had reproached herself for her foolishness, her unthinking impulsiveness, the sexual irresponsibility that could have landed her in the worst mess she had ever experienced in her life—but never as much as she was doing now. And all the reproofs she had thrown at herself in the darkness of the night were as nothing when compared to the dark scorn, the bitter contempt that burned in Gio's dark eyes as he fixed them on her flushed and uneasy face.

'It was only one night.'

'Madre de Dio!' The words seemed to be torn from

Gio's lips, his exclamation a sound of such deep disgust that it ripped into her already vulnerable heart like a deadly sharp stiletto. The wound that it left behind was so deep, so cruel, that she was desperately afraid it would ultimately prove fatal, even though right now the shock and the savagery of it had caused the blessed oblivion of numbness.

'It only takes one *time*.'

'I know that! I'm not a fool!'

The blazingly scathing glare he turned on her told her that a fool was the least insulting thing he wanted to call her, the heat of his contempt searing dangerously over her exposed skin.

'Then don't act like one! Face facts! You might be pregnant—and if you are then we have to decide what to do about it!'

'*I* have to decide what to do about it!'

'It would be my child!'

'Only half yours!'

But even as she flung the words into his dark face, she knew them for the mistake they were. To Giovanni Cardella, pure, unreformed Sicilian male, any child he fathered was *his* and no one else's. The woman who was given the honour of being impregnated by his seed might just get some consideration while she was carrying and nurturing the precious child, but once it was born it would be pure Cardella and nothing else. Then she might be lucky enough to be allowed a look-in on its upbringing, but little more. Unless, of course, she was the saintly Lucia.

'But I would take care of it. I would make sure it had everything it needed growing up. I—'

'I could do that as well!'

'How? Where?'

Flinging his hands up in a supremely Italian gesture, Gio spun on his heel, dark eyes surveying the small, scruffy room with its well-worn furniture.

'In some other shabby, run-down mouse hole like this? Where there's no garden, nowhere for a child to play? No space to run around? And how would you support it? You don't even have enough money to keep yourself—or were you expecting your parents to take care of your child as well as you?'

'No! Never!'

'Then what did you plan to do?'

'I don't know...' It was low and miserable, just a whisper of defeat. How could she claim she'd made any plans when the truth was that the fear she might be pregnant had run round and round in her head during the past week? And each time it had haunted her thoughts she had struggled to think what to do if she was, but never, ever come to any conclusions.

'I don't know. I didn't think.'

'You didn't think,' Gio echoed darkly. 'You can say that again. Well, will you at least make the effort to think now?'

'I'm not giving you my baby!'

'Did I ask you to?'

With an obvious effort he adjusted his tone down a degree or two, imposing a ruthless control that calmed his voice, softened its intonation.

'We don't even know if you're pregnant yet—but we have to consider the possibility. All I ask is that you come to Sicily with me so that I can keep an eye on you, at least until things become clear one way or another. You'll be well cared for, looked after.'

'Supervised to make sure that I don't do anything to harm your child, don't you mean? Or, even worse, sleep with someone else and then try to pass off their bastard as a pure-bred Cardella.'

Fury flared in Gio's eyes at her bitter comment, but he didn't even deign to honour it with a reply.

'Call it a free holiday if you like,' he tossed at her. 'You said it was a long time since you had one of those. Perhaps that will make the whole thing more appealing.'

A holiday, Terrie thought longingly. The idea was more than appealing. It sounded *wonderful*. A holiday in Sicily—with sun and the sea, and Gio...

Ten minutes ago, she would have snatched his hand off.

But then ten minutes ago she had still been a poor, blind, deluded fool, lost in the fantasy that he cared—at least enough to want her with him for some time.

Well, he still wanted her with him—but for his own selfish reasons.

'So will you come?'

He had to be joking!

'It seems an eminently sensible solution to me. You can stay in my home for a month—just four short weeks. And if at the end of that time we know you're not pregnant then you can go on your way and there'll be no further complications.'

'And if I *am* pregnant?' Terrie forced herself to ask, willing her insides not to curdle sourly at that 'no further complications'. 'What happens then?'

'We'll decide when we have some facts to act on. Who knows, by then we might find that the answer's taken care of itself?'

'That we get on so well together that we want to stay that way for the baby's sake? Don't bank on it!'

Terrie prayed that the shake in her voice could be taken as having been put there by laughter at just the thought of the two of them ever wanting to decide that. At least that way it might somehow conceal the pain that tore at her inside, the sudden longing to be able to believe that it could happen. That if they had time together they might just grow close, come to feel more for each other.

'Stranger things have happened.'

'But not to me.'

'I'm not looking for another love of my life—I already had that with Lucia, and lightning doesn't strike twice.'

'If you're trying to persuade me that we could have a future together, then you're going exactly the wrong way about it!'

Did he know how much it hurt to know that she would always be second best to his beloved dead wife? That he had wanted Lucia for love, but the only reason he wanted her was because she might be carrying his child?

'What makes you think that this would work?'

'Why not? We get on well enough together in bed. More than well enough. That has to count for something.'

'And sex is the answer to all of this?'

'It's a damned good place to start.'

And the only one, his expression said. The one and only thing she gave him that he couldn't live without. Any dream she had had of finding that there was more to the way he was feeling shrivelled into a microscopic pile of dust on the floor at her feet.

But almost immediately foolish hope reasserted itself. Perhaps there *was* a chance. If she went along with Gio's plan then maybe, just maybe, as they spent the days together they could get to know each other better, grow closer—at least closer on his part. Perhaps they might come to, if not a love relationship, then at least an understanding—and from an understanding something more could grow, given time.

And Gio had offered her time.

Only four weeks, it was true. But it was better than nothing. Better than watching him walk out of here once more and knowing that this time he would never come back.

She could give it a try. She *had* to give it a try. After all, what did she have to lose—how could she come out of it with any less than what she had now? And there might just be the faintest chance that she could end up with more.

'So…' Gio's voice broke into her thoughts. 'What's your answer? Are you coming with me?'

His swift glance at his watch told her that he was already thinking impatiently of leaving and the things he had to do before he got on the plane. She had to make her mind up and she had to do it fast.

'All right,' Terrie said cautiously. 'I'll do it.'

The look in his eyes gave him away. He might have schooled his expression into the cool, noncommittal mask that met her anxious gaze, but he couldn't disguise the flare of triumph, the sexual satisfaction that gleamed in the ebony darkness.

'Bene!'

He was taking a step towards her, his intention to kiss her evident. But that was a move too far. Terrie had been caught that way once already. She had no intention of letting it happen again.

Instinctively she held up her hand, bringing him to a reluctant halt.

'One condition!'

His swift sidelong glance told her that she was in no position to go laying down conditions, but to her relief he paused and nodded slowly.

'And that is?'

'While we're in Sicily it's strictly hands off! Is that understood?'

It was clearly the last thing he had expected and the black, arched brows shot up in evident surprise.

'Is that so?'

'Yes!'

She prayed she sounded more confident than she felt. The mocking note in his voice, the devilish look in his eye, both set her nerves on edge and made her wonder just what she had taken on.

'Hands off?'

He was coming towards her with the slow, deliberate prowl of a hunting cat; gleaming eyes fixed on her face.

'Y-yes…'

Definitely not so sure this time. And even though she had taken several hasty steps backwards, his steady advance seemed to be gaining on her.

'Is that a challenge, *cara*?'

A challenge? Now she was totally bemused. How could he take her total rejection of his advances as a challenge to something more?

She soon learned. A moment later her backwards movement was halted as first her foot, and then her shoulders came up against the wall. There was nowhere she could go. And Gio was still coming closer.

'Gio…'

She tried to make his name a sound of warning, but knew she had either failed or was being totally ignored as he came even closer, moving right in front of her, trapping her in the corner with the bulk of his body.

'Hands off, hmm? Well, fine, if that's the way you want it, *carina*. But there are plenty of other ways…'

She could read what was coming from the look in his eyes and frantically turned her face to left and right, trying to avoid him. But Gio imprisoned her by pressing the hard length of his body up against hers—his hands firmly down by his sides, while, as she had anticipated, his mouth sought hers.

And there was no way she could avoid his kiss. Even though she twisted this way and that, she knew he would defeat her soon. In the end it came sooner than she had expected, because when he saw that she was determined to resist him he gave up on the direct approach, and went for a more subtle form of enticement. Terrie's heart jumped in startled reaction as she felt the warmth of his mouth at the base of her neck, lingering softly on the point where her frantic pulse raced. And even as she stilled, unable to do anything but relax into enjoyment of the caress, he started to move, kissing his way slowly up and over her sensitive skin.

'There are more ways to make love to a woman than with your hands, *belleza*,' he murmured against her quivering flesh. 'More ways to caress than by touching...'

And as Terrie froze into immobility, unable to resist, to fight the sensations that were sparking through her, he proceeded to demonstrate exactly what he meant.

He used his mouth like a delicate instrument of pleasure, smoothing, kissing, lapping at her skin. He even made one or two delicate, nipping little bites that had her crying out, in spite of the efforts she made to bite her lip against the betraying sound.

He kissed his way up the slender line of her throat, traced the line of her jaw where a muscle she couldn't control jumped in frantic response. He trailed his tongue around the coils of her ear, sending shivers of reaction through each connecting delicate nerve, and so to every sensitised part of her body. His lips pressed her eyelids shut so that the enforced darkness heightened every sensation she was experiencing, and it was only when she was a pliant, quivering wreck of uncontrolled response that he finally took her mouth in a deep, impassioned and demanding kiss.

'Open to me, *adorata*,' he murmured against her softening lips. 'Open to me and let me show you how a man kisses the woman whose image has haunted his dreams, kept him from sleeping, kept him from eating... The woman who is driving him crazy...'

She *meant* to fight him. Terrie told herself that she wanted to resist...but her body had other ideas. Her bones seemed to melt, her knees buckling weakly in the heat of the desire that seared along every nerve. She could only be grateful for the solidity of the wall at her back, the pressure of Gio's mouth against hers that held her head still and upright.

And still he hadn't touched her; his hands were braced firmly against the paintwork, a couple of feet from her body on either side.

And that was not what she wanted. Her body was aching, yearning, demanding. Her breasts seemed swollen, heavy and full, just wanting—needing the caress of those long, knowing fingers, the heat of his palms against their peaking nipples. But Gio was resolute, ruthless in his control, using only his mouth to pleasure her. And that pleasure, combined with the subtle cruelty of his control, only made her want him all the more desperately.

'Gio...'

His name was a sigh of surrender and a cry of protest all at once, and she strained her hungry body away from the wall, needing the pressure of his against it, the heat and hardness of his strength tight against her hungry flesh. A second, choking cry was torn from her as Gio, with a smile she could feel against her skin, slid his mouth away from her lips, heading down this time. Down to where the low-scooped neckline of her T-shirt just skimmed the top of the curves of her breasts, the faint pressure of his kiss, the tantalising warmth of his breath making her writhe in a tormented frustration of desire.

'Oh, Gio…' she gasped again and felt his smile grow wide, wicked, fiendish.

The next moment his mouth was against her shoulder, his tongue tracing erotic patterns all the way to where the soft pink cotton of her sleeve began. Hard white teeth fixed on the stretchy material, tugging softly, edging it away and down…

And it was too much for her to take any longer. She couldn't bear the sensory deprivation and the seductive torment he was subjecting her to at one and the same time.

'Oh, my…*Gio*!'

Unthinkingly, blindly she reached for him, wanting to close her arms around his neck, tangle her hungry fingers in the coal-black silk of his hair. Needing…

But Gio reacted swiftly and sharply, snapping his head up and twisting himself away from her grasping hands, breaking all physical contact with her, stepping firmly back, well out of reach.

'No touching!' he said, his tone as cold as his eyes. 'Hands off, *belleza*, that's what you said. You made the rules…'

And now she wanted to break them. The agonisingly sharp arousal he had sparked off all over her body was screaming out for appeasement and she felt that she would shatter into a million tiny fragments if he didn't take her back into his arms once more and hold her tight, kiss away the clamouring distress.

She even held out her hands towards him, wanting, needing, hoping to encourage him to come back to her and finish what he had started. But Gio neatly sidestepped her reaching arms, smoothing down his ruffled hair and straightening his clothing with brisk, coolly efficient movements.

'Hands off,' he repeated, his tone cold and clipped, and then to Terrie's total consternation he actually smiled deep into her eyes.

At least, his mouth smiled, but there was no warmth, no trace of humour in it. And his own dark-eyed gaze remained cool and opaque, impenetrable as polished marble.

'Your rules, *cara mia*. That's the way you wanted to play it.'

Terrie could find no words to answer him. None, at least, that she was prepared to give any sort of voice to. If she opened her mouth, she knew that she would be forced to beg. Beg him to come back to her, to hold her, kiss her, caress her. To take her to bed and make sweet, savage, passionate love to her until she was mindless and melting in fulfilment.

And she didn't dare admit that to him. Because it meant admitting the effect he had on her, the power he held over her. She suspected that that was something he knew already. But at least if she didn't actually *say* it then she hadn't put the weapon into his hands, giving him something he could use against her whenever he wanted.

And so she remained stubbornly silent, though her whole body trembled with the effort that it cost her to keep her lips clamped shut, her mouth sealed against the weak words of surrender that struggled to escape her.

For a long, silent moment Gio's dark eyes rested on her face, taking in every inch of her colourless cheeks, her quivering mouth, her over-bright eyes. And then just as she was nerving herself for some other onslaught, one she was afraid her weakened defences would be incapable of repelling, suddenly, shockingly, he smiled again.

'My plane leaves at five,' he said, his tone disturbingly matter-of-fact. 'I'll be here to collect you a couple of hours before that. I expect you to be packed and ready to leave.'

Terrie still could find no reply to give him, but he made it clear that he wasn't expecting one, turning on his heel and striding towards the door. With his fingers on the handle, turning it, he stilled and half turned back to her, dark eyes like lasers probing into her soul.

'You made the rules, *carina*, so you have only yourself to blame if you don't like the way things work out. While I'm gone, perhaps you might like to rethink the way you want to play this.'

A moment later he was gone, and, released at last from the tension that was all that had been holding her upright, Terrie gave a raw, choking gasp and let go, sliding all the way down the wall to collapse in a weak, shaken heap on the floor. Too exhausted, too shattered even to cry, she could only bury her face in her hands and moan aloud as she gave herself up to the pain of her despair.

CHAPTER TEN

'TREEZA! Treeza! Looka me!'

Obedient to Paolo's shrieked command, using his own personal version of her name, Terrie looked across to the opposite side of the swimming pool to where the little boy was poised on the edge of the tiled surround.

'Go on, then!' she encouraged. 'Jump!'

Tanned arms and legs waving frantically, Paolo launched himself into the air and landed, with the maximum amount of splashing, in the cool blue water just a short distance from her. Laughing, Terrie slid back into the cool water and made her way in a leisurely breaststroke to the spot where he had surfaced, spluttering wildly, a wide, brilliant grin on his face.

'See me?' he spluttered, wiping the streaming water away from his eyes and nose. 'See me jump?'

'I saw you,' Terrie told him. 'I don't think anyone could miss you.'

It really wasn't fair, she reflected. Surely nature could have arranged it so that Gio's son hadn't been quite such a perfect replica of his father. His hair, his eyes, his features, all were a smaller, younger copy of his father's, so that even when Gio wasn't actually around at the villa then Paolo was always there to remind her of him, the man faithfully reflected in the boy.

Not that she could ever *forget* what Gio was like, she admitted ruefully. It seemed that he was always in her mind, always at the forefront of her thoughts, and she had only to close her eyes, or simply to think of him, and an image of his dark, stunning features rose before her, clear as life, without a second's hesitation.

'Ride! Ride!'

Paolo was bouncing up and down in the water, sending rippling waves radiating out towards the sides. Gio had insisted that his son be brought up speaking both English and Italian, and he managed to communicate well enough in Terrie's own language when he was with her.

'Treeza—pleeese!'

'A piggyback ride? Again? Oh, OK…'

She couldn't deny this little boy anything. From the first moment that she had been introduced to him, Paolo had stolen a part of her heart away, and she knew she would never get it back. And it seemed that he felt the same about her. Certainly, he loved to be in her company, and after only a moment or two's wary shyness he had taken to her as if he had known her all his life.

She turned her back on him, lowering herself until her shoulders were covered in the water, and he could climb onto her back. When Paolo's arms were tight around her neck, his sturdy legs clamped about her waist, she kicked off and swam, slowly and carefully because of her precious burden, from one side of the pool to another.

From the far side of the terrace, hidden in the shade of the house, Gio stilled on his way to the pool, and watched the scene before him in unmoving silence.

Terrie's blonde hair was slicked wetly against the fine bones of her skull, and her long, slender arms stroked through the water with smooth, powerful movements. Clinging on to her shoulders like a limpet, his son was beaming in total delight, his wide, bright smile as brilliant as the afternoon sunlight.

'Go, Treeza, go, go!'

The little boy's voice, shrill with excitement, echoed all

around the wide, high terrace, and as he heard it something clenched inside Gio's heart, twisting it sharply and painfully.

Madre de Dio, just what was happening to him? Was he jealous of his own son?

And why should it surprise him that the answer was yes? Wasn't it the case that from the moment he had introduced Paolo to Terrie, he had openly envied the little boy's unrestrained ease and uncomplicated friendship with the beautiful blonde?

Face it, he told himself. He was frankly jealous of Terrie's relationship with every member of his family.

She had charmed the entire Cardella clan, effortlessly winning over first his stepfather and then his mother. And even Gio's half-brother Cesare was entranced by her, while Cesare's wife Megan had taken to the newcomer as if they had been sisters separated at birth.

And what made matters so much worse was the fact that since he had brought Teresa to Sicily she had stuck rigidly to her 'hands off' policy. In fact, from the time that he had arrived at her flat to collect her on the start of their journey to Italy, she seemed to have changed into some other woman entirely. A cool-voiced, cool-eyed, cool-natured creature, who forced him to doubt whether the hotly responsive, passionate lover he had taken to bed on their first—their only—night together had ever truly existed or was just a figment of his imagination.

But then as he watched, Terrie reached the far end of the swimming pool, lifted Paolo out, and then hoisted herself onto the white tiled edge beside him. With unconscious grace she tossed back her soaking hair, stretching lightly in the sun, and immediately his senses kicked into overdrive, need clawing at him cruelly.

A week in the warmth of Sicily had brought a light,

golden tone to her skin, drawing out silvery highlights in the blonde of her hair. And the simple, beautifully cut, deep turquoise swimming costume clung in all the right places, smoothing and enhancing the sleek curves of her body and exposing long, long legs and elegantly slender arms. When she bent down to rub at Paolo's hair with the white towel the sight of the delicate line of her neck and shoulder caught on something raw deep inside him, making him clamp his teeth down hard into his bottom lip to hold back the groan of animal response that almost escaped him.

Dannazione, but he was finding this 'hands off' rule impossible to live with!

A week ago it had been a matter of pride for Gio to stick with it absolutely, never once even laying a finger on her. She would come to him, he had vowed. She would break before he did. And he had taken a sort of perverse pleasure in making sure he followed the ruling to the limit. At least as far as his *hands* were concerned.

His arms might brush against hers, his leg came close to the length of her thigh when they sat together. He made sure that he kissed her at each meeting or parting, and his body often brushed against her when they met in a corridor or had to pass in a doorway. But, in all the time since they had left her flat on the journey here, never once had any part of his hands touched any part of her body.

'*Papa!*'

Paolo had caught sight of him, wriggling free from Terrie's gentle restraint and running towards his father, smile wide and brilliant, arms outstretched.

'*Papa! Papa!*'

'*Ciao, bambino!*'

Gio caught the sturdy little body in both hands, lifting his son and swinging him high in the air, his smile as bright as Paolo's as he looked up into the small, laughing face.

'And how is my little one today? What have you been up to?'

'I swim!' Paolo crowed jubilantly. '*Papa*, I swim with Treeza!'

'You sweem?' Gio echoed, laughter bubbling up in his voice as he echoed his son's imperfect English pronunciation. 'Did you indeed? Are you sure you swam...?'

To Terrie's total consternation his gleaming dark eyes slid to her face in a swift, amusement-filled glance that brought her into a joking conspiracy with him, the gesture so warm, so intimate that it made her heart lurch in instant response.

'Because when I saw you it was Teresa who was doing all the sweeming, and you were having a ride!'

'*Papa*—no!'

In his flurry of protest, all Paolo's English deserted him and he subjected his father to a tirade in chirpy Italian that only made Gio's smile widen even more, until at last he threw back his head and laughed out loud, relaxing totally into his feelings in a way that Terrie had rarely seen him do before.

Swamped by a rush of disturbing sensation, a flood of heat that filled her veins from head to toe, making her whole body glow in a way that had nothing to do with the warmth of the sun, Terrie swiftly turned away, unable to watch any longer. Snatching up her towel, she rubbed it fiercely against her face, more as a way of concealing her expression, hiding the betraying colour of her cheeks, than in any attempt to dry her skin. Already the sunny afternoon had made the lingering moisture evaporate, and even the material of her swimming costume was drying so fast that she might never have been in the pool at all.

'OK, so you swam. I believe you.'

The laughter was still there in Gio's voice, sparking off sensations in her thoughts that complicated her already intense reactions to him.

She had to drag her eyes away from the way that Gio's strong hands held his small son so gently yet so securely, long, tanned fingers splayed out against the olive-toned flesh of the small torso. Needed to wipe from her mind the memories of the pleasure just the touch of those hands could bring, the tingling sensation that lingered where they had smoothed her hair, caressed her skin.

When she had agreed to come here to Sicily with him, she had been so sure that she could keep to the crazily impulsive 'hands off' rule that she had flung at him in a temper on that afternoon in her flat. She had had some vague sort of thought that perhaps if Gio found that she wasn't as freely available for sex as he had seemed to expect then he might find other reasons for being with her, other pleasures that her company might bring. She had even hoped that it might just be a case of abstinence making the heart grow fonder.

But she had been sorely disappointed. Gio had seemed worryingly unmoved. He had made none of the sarcastic or critical comments she had anticipated. In fact, he had said nothing at all. And on their arrival here at the villa he had made no attempt to persuade her to share his room, but instead had led her to a totally separate room at the far end of the corridor to his. In fact, she had been forced to wonder whether she had had any effect on him. And, even worse, she had been obliged to ask herself if *she* was the one who was suffering most as a result of her own impetuous edict.

And she had reckoned without the way that the very different climate and way of life that Gio knew in his native land had changed the man himself. In ways that only deepened and dangerously enhanced his already potent sexual attraction until it was positively lethal to any sort of peace of mind she might have hoped for.

Here, in the warmth of the sun, and with the relaxed pace of life enjoyed in his island villa, the sophisticated city lawyer had disappeared, and in his place was a more relaxed, far more casual Giovanni Cardella than she had ever believed existed. Gone were the sleek city suits and in their place were loose T-shirts and shorts that exposed the muscular length of his legs. And several times he had joined Terrie and Paolo for a swim, sending her pulse rate rocketing when he stripped off to reveal the toned lines of a body that the sun had tanned to the shade of dark bronze.

She was desperately afraid that if she stayed in Sicily much longer, he would come to mean more to her than it was safe for her to feel.

Not that she *could* feel any more.

The thought slammed into her mind with the force of a blow to her head, making her reel dizzily.

Where had that come from? And was it true? As soon as she asked herself the question she knew there was only one answer.

She had no way of escape, she told herself. No matter what rational controls she tried to impose on it, her body recognised the personal sexual brand this man had set on it on their single night together. A secret brand that made her as much his possession as if she had been bought and sold in a slave market in days gone by. And she would always be held by that bond, no matter how hard she might struggle to get away.

If she could have done so without provoking suspicion she would have tossed aside the towel and plunged back into the blue depths of the pool, wanting to have them close over her head, conceal her from Gio's prying eyes. She longed for the shock of the cool water against her heated body, dousing and controlling the pounding blood in her veins, the ache of need that was uncoiling low down in the cradle of her pelvis.

'But now it's time for you to go inside,' Gio was saying, lowering his son slowly and setting his small bare feet safely on the ground.

'No!'

Paolo's small face set into stubborn lines that made him look unnervingly like his father. 'I stay with Treeza! I love Treeza! Treeza—love 'oo.'

Teresa sensed rather than saw Gio's sudden stiffening, but she didn't dare to look into his face to see the effect his son's innocent words were having on him. Never before had she felt the ambiguity of her position in Gio's household as strongly as she did now. Admitting to cowardice, she concentrated fiercely on the little boy.

'And I love you, sweetie. But you must do as your daddy says. If he says it's time to go in...'

'And Nonna is here,' Gio added, forestalling the protest Paolo was obviously about to make. 'She's waiting to see you.'

The bribe worked. Paolo adored his paternal grandmother. His smile restored, he set off at a fast pace, heading for the big patio doors into the house.

Gio watched him go, waiting until he saw his son safely indoors before he turned back to Terrie.

'You're a strong swimmer,' he commented, though Terrie had a firm feeling that he was speaking to say anything, fill the silence, with his mind not on the subject he had raised at all. 'Where did you learn?'

·'My mother taught me. She loved the water. And then at school I was in the competition team.'

She was hunting for her cover-up as she spoke, finding the loose cotton shirt on a sun-lounger near by. The sense of relief with which she shrugged it on was ridiculous, she knew. The fine weave of the white cotton made the garment almost totally transparent anyway, and at best it was a concession to modesty, nothing more. It certainly wasn't any protection from the dark, assessing gaze that roved over her body in the clinging swimsuit with evident approval.

'Did Lucia like to swim?'

She wouldn't have asked the question if she hadn't already been off balance. Since her arrival at the villa, Lucia Cardella had been a forbidden topic between them. It was impossible to ignore the photographs of the petite, dark-haired woman that were scattered around the large, elegant rooms, but Gio's first wife had never actually been discussed. So now she froze in apprehension, wondering if perhaps she had overstepped some unseen barrier, crossed a line that she didn't even know was there.

'No, she hated it,' he said slowly. 'As a matter of fact, she was terrified of water. Her father was one of those who believed that the way to overcome a nervous fear is to confront it head-on. So, when he saw her hesitating on the side of the pool as a child, he picked her up and threw her in.'

'Oh, poor Lucia. That would just make matters worse!'

'It did.'

Gio's voice was low and flat, dull as his eyes. He seemed to be staring out across the rippling water of the pool, his gaze unfocused, and Terrie had the feeling that he was looking back into his past, reliving some memory. Her heart twisted at the thought of his loss, the loneliness of his life since, and, reacting automatically, she reached out and laid a gentle hand on his arm.

'I'm sorry—I shouldn't have…'

Gio started brusquely at her touch, his hazed eyes going sharply to her face. For a couple of blank seconds it was as if he didn't recognise her, as he stared straight through her, then he blinked hard and came back to himself.

That had never happened before, Gio realised. Terrie had asked him a question about Lucia and it was only when she had that he had realised that his wife, while still so vivid in his memories, had actually not been uppermost in his thoughts. For a second or two he had had to hunt for the facts he wanted to answer her question.

'Non c'e problema,' he muttered automatically. 'It's fine.'

But then he looked down at her hand, small and delicate, as it lay on his arm. In the sunlight the scent of her skin was an evocative perfume, one that stirred his senses to a demanding throb.

'What happened to "hands off"?' he queried softly, lacing the words with a touch of wry amusement.

'Oh, that…'

For the space of a couple of heartbeats, Terrie looked nonplussed, but then swiftly she recovered, even shot him a provocatively challenging glance from the corners of her eyes.

'I only said "hands off" to you! Nowhere is it written that the rule applies to me!'

'You little witch!'

He made it a low, rolling growl, the sound of a dozing tiger, half-roused from sleep, but too lazily contented to bother with pouncing. He was still having trouble adjusting to the discovery he had made about himself just moments before.

'But perhaps it's just as well that there is some contact between us. My mother was starting to wonder just what sort of a couple we are…'

'You told her we are—a couple?'

It was her turn to look disconcerted and she snatched her hand back as if the slight connection between them had burned her, making her flinch away.

'*Naturalmente.*'

'But then—won't she think it's odd that we don't share…that we aren't…?'

'Sleeping together?'

A quick, ironic smile tugged at the corners of his mouth at the memory of his conversation with his mother earlier that week.

'Not at all, *cara mia*. This is Sicily, remember. Mama is still old-fashioned enough to approve of the fact that we have separate rooms. She believes that it is a sign of how serious we are about each other—that I treat you with such respect.'

'And so how will you explain it if I am pregnant?'

'My mother is a realist. She knows that the behaviour she admires here is not necessarily the same everywhere else. Besides, she has always dreamed of having more grandchildren, and now that Cesare and Megan are about to present her with a new member of the family she is hoping to see her dream come true. She would not worry if a baby was conceived before marriage—just as long as it was born into a properly formalised relationship.'

'Marriage?' Terrie looked stunned. 'We didn't discuss marriage.'

'We didn't discuss it, but you must have realised that it was the obvious solution if you should turn out to be carrying my child.'

'Not that obvious to me!'

It was as if a violent thunderstorm was brewing inside her head, making Terrie's thoughts spin.

Marriage. To Gio. How would she feel about that?

The question had knocked her completely off balance, but it was the answer that sent her spinning over the edge and into a freefall of panic-stricken shock.

She couldn't think of anything that she would like better. Couldn't imagine anything more terrifyingly wonderful than the prospect of waking up every day, for the rest of her existence, and knowing that Gio was there, in her life—that this devastating, stunning, sexy man was her *husband*.

'I didn't think—'

'Then *think*!' Gio ordered curtly. 'Any day now we will know. And when we know we will have to act. If you are *incinta*, then the sooner we announce our proposed union the better.'

The spiralling freefall of confusion had ended by dropping her, mentally at least, into an ice-cold pond, sobering her up fast. While she had been thinking of togetherness and a future filled with the time to get to know this man properly, to share his life, his home, his bed, Gio's thoughts had all been of practicalities. Of making public their 'proposed union', for all the world as if it was to be nothing but a legal deal he had thrashed out in court.

But why should that surprise her? It was, after all, the only way Gio actually thought about the possibility of their marriage. He had made that plain before they had left England, telling her in no uncertain terms that he had no heart left to give to her.

'I'm not looking for another love of my life,' he had said. 'I already had that with Lucia, and lightning doesn't strike twice.'

'And how would your mother feel about that?'

'She is delighted that I have a new woman in my life. She believes that it is not good for a man to live alone.'

And any woman was better than none. Any woman would fill the space in his bed, in his house, in his life—but not in his heart. He didn't have to say the words; they were there in his tone, in the opaque look in his eyes.

'It was my mother who sent me out to you here. She is concerned that you and I are not getting any time alone together because of Paolo, and so she has offered to have him all day tomorrow—and all night too. He loves to sleep at her house so he'll see it as a real treat. And we can go out and I can show you the island.'

'That's kind of her.'

Terrie's response was abstracted. Her whirling brain had picked on one phrase and held on to it like a terrier fastening on to a slipper.

'All day…and all night'.

It was crazy to let that fix in her thoughts and mean so much more than the simple phrase deserved, but she couldn't stop herself from doing so. All week, she and Gio had been alone in the house—apart from the small, innocent person of Paolo. A totally empty house, other than the two of them, wouldn't be so very different—would it?

And yet somehow she felt as if it would be completely unlike every other day she had already spent in the villa.

'A full day without any parental responsibilities,' Gio murmured. 'It would be a pity to waste it.'

'Mm.'

It was all that Terrie could manage. She didn't dare to ask him just what he meant by 'waste'. She already had some very strong suspicions as to what was behind the apparently innocent remark. And with her own newly recognised feelings still raw in her mind, she was not at all sure that she would be able to cope with the implications of that.

A full day without any parental responsibilities, Gio reflected. And who knew just how things might stand between them at the end of that day?

Twenty-four hours in which, for the first time in this upside-down relationship, they would actually have a chance to do things the conventional way—follow the usual path that most couples took.

Most male-female relationships started with liking, moved to love, and from there to the deep passion of a committed future together. That was how things had been with Lucia. He had liked her the moment he had seen her; known he loved her in the blink of an eye after that, it had seemed. Had wanted them to be together for the rest of their lives, but it was not to be.

And they had waited what had seemed like an eternity before they slept together.

None of which fitted the way things had developed with Teresa. Instead he had felt as if a tornado had swept into his life, picked him up and whirled him far from anywhere he recognised, losing track of all the familiar landmarks he had ever known. And when he had finally been set down again, he had no idea whether he was on his head or his heels. He only knew that he couldn't get this woman out of his mind. That without her in his life he felt as if he was losing his grip on his sanity.

But when she was with him, he couldn't work out what he wanted with her.

Perhaps tomorrow would give him a chance to get things back under control again. Maybe twenty-four hours from now, he would have some idea of just exactly where he went from here.

And whether Teresa came with him or not.

CHAPTER ELEVEN

THE sun had gone down completely by the time that they returned to the villa late the following evening. After their day out they had had dinner at a wonderful restaurant in Palermo, before making their way back along the winding country roads to Gio's home. Already the heat of the day had chilled to a cool, still evening, and in the darkness the house seemed incredibly silent and empty.

'It seems strange not to have to keep quiet for fear of waking Paolo,' Terrie said as they made their way into the huge lounge. 'Was he always such a light sleeper?'

'Not for the first year.'

Gio tossed his car keys onto the sideboard and went to stand by the patio doors, staring out at the terrace where the pool lay empty and almost still, just a few tiny waves, stirred by a faint wind, lapping lazily at the sides.

'Until he was twelve months old, he slept so deeply that it would have taken an earthquake to waken him. But then things changed. After...'

'After Lucia...' Terrie inserted softly, sensing intuitively the words that had deserted him as his shoulders tensed, and one hand covered his eyes. 'That's what you mean, isn't it? Young as he was, Paolo sensed that someone very special was missing from his life.'

And, from the way that the little boy who had known his mother only such a short time had reacted, she could guess at how deeply his father, who had loved her as much as life itself, had felt her loss.

'Yeah...'

It was a long-drawn-out sigh, one that wrenched at her heart, brought the sting of tears to her eyes.

'That's exactly what I mean.'

Abruptly he swung round, turning to face her, and on a shock of surprise Terrie suddenly had the strangest feeling that he was looking at her almost as if for the first time.

'I hope you enjoyed yourself today.'

'I had a wonderful time!' Terrie answered with total honesty, knowing that the gleam in her eyes must speak for itself. 'I've never been that close to the site of a volcano before.'

The circular journey to Etna had been like a pattern of light and shade. In the foothills of the great volcano were the richness of the olive groves, the glistening citrus and the nut plantations. But clinging to the sides of Etna itself had been dark volcanic villages and ruined Norman castles. Further up, seen from a cable car, the setting had seemed like nothing so much as a moonscape.

'It's a scary place.' She gave a shiver just remembering. 'But I'm glad I've seen it. What was that name you said that native Sicilians call Etna?'

'Mongibello. It comes from the Arabic for mountain. Some people just call it *a muntagna*—the mountain—pure and simple.'

Gio's tone was vague and distracted. It was clear that his attention was not on the subject at all.

'Would you like a drink?' Terrie asked, feeling awkward and unsure of herself.

The trip out had gone so well. Gio had seemed relaxed and at ease, a charming and knowledgeable guide to the places they had visited, and an easy, entertaining companion over dinner. But since they had come back into the house it was as if unease had settled round her like a cloak, coming between her and the comfortable mood of the day.

'Some wine?'

'No, nothing alcoholic.'

Gio shook his head. He wanted nothing that might cloud his mind, stop him from thinking clearly. All day he had been plagued by the strangest feelings, ones he didn't know how to handle, and anything intoxicating could only make matters so much worse. It was almost as if he was standing outside himself, watching every move he made, and not understanding it.

He had walked through familiar places, seen familiar sights. He had even eaten in a long-time favourite restaurant. Somewhere where he'd been perhaps a hundred times or more. And everything had seemed new and strangely different.

And he had felt differently too.

The only way he could describe it was that the empty space at his side—the space that he had lived with all day and every day for the last two years—suddenly seemed to be not so empty, not so dark.

It wasn't just that he had had someone with him. He'd lost count of how many times he had gone to some of the special places he had shared with Lucia—alone, with Cesare or Megan, or even the two of them together *and* Paolo. And still he had felt empty, lost and alone.

Today the tall, slender figure of a blonde Englishwoman had gone a long way towards filling that space. And in a way that no one else ever could.

Teresa... He had opened his mouth to say her name, to tell her...but then the realisation that he didn't know *what* to tell her closed his lips again, just as Terrie, enticing, laughed suddenly.

'Well, I'd offer to make you some coffee, if you think

we'd drink it this time. That night in the hotel, and again in my flat, it just got left untouched and went cold. Third time lucky, do you think?'

Gio found that to his surprise the smile that was needed in response came unexpectedly easily, sharing in her amusement.

'So long as we don't risk the brandy as well.'

'No brandy, I promise you.' Terrie laughed again, leading the way out of the lounge and across the tiled hallway.

In the kitchen, Gio leaned against the pale wood cabinets, watching her as she moved around, intent on the simple task. She looked like a pale, exotic flower in a simple sleeveless dress the same shade of turquoise as the swimming costume she had worn yesterday, but so many tones lighter that it looked as if it had faded over time, washed to something very close to white.

Because of the warmth of the day she had caught her hair up in a neat coil at the base of her skull and as she bent her head over the cafetière, concentrating on measuring the right amount of coffee grounds, the delicacy and vulnerability of the curve of her neck affected him strongly.

He felt the clutch of desire deep inside. But at the same time he also felt a rush of gentleness, a fiercely protective rush of emotion that made his head spin with its sheer power.

Unable to stop himself, he moved forward, coming behind her, and dropped a soft, lingering kiss on the exposed skin at the top of her spine.

'Mm...'

Her response was soft and sensual, like a small cat's purr. But then she twisted round to face him, looking deep into his eyes, a faintly puzzled frown creasing the space between her brows.

'What was that for?'

'Because I wanted to. And you can't complain because…'

He lifted both his hands and spread them out on either side of her, bronzed fingers splayed wide.

'See…no hands.'

To Terrie's intense relief there was no darkness in his tone, no underlying thread of anger or reproach. Instead there was a lightness and humour that amazed her, relaxing the strain of muscles held taut with uncertainty.

'I'll let you off, then,' she returned on a matching note, then, drawing in a deep, strengthening breath, she seized the chance his mood had given her. 'Would it help to talk about it? About Lucia?'

She fully expected rejection. Was sure that he would close up, turn against her, or at least tell her it was none of her business. But instead he sighed, flexing his shoulders under the silver-grey silk jacket, and said, 'What do you want to know?'

Terrie swallowed hard, unsure of how to answer that.

'Whatever you want to tell me.'

Gio swung away from her again, but to her relief she saw that it was not to reject her, but so that he could pace up and down the big farmhouse-style kitchen, his restless movements obviously reflecting the unsettled nature of his thoughts.

'We were both only sixteen when we met…'

His voice sounded cracked and rusty, as if it was a long time since it had been used, and he was clearly not finding it easy to use the right words to express his memories. Terrie longed to go to him, to hold him, to help him, but she sensed intuitively that this was not the right moment. Gio needed to handle this on his own. Later, when he had finished, that would be the time to go to him and try to comfort him.

If he would let her.

'I took one look at her and I just *knew*.'

Gio paused in his restless pacing for just a second, pushed both hands through his hair, staring into space as if picturing the scene, then launched into movement once again.

'Cesare always says that the men in our family fall heavily when they fall in love. That it's a once-in-a-lifetime sort of thing...'

Terrie could only be grateful that as the words left his mouth Gio was at the far end of the kitchen, where his long, restless strides had taken him. His back was to her and so he never saw the way that she flinched at his words, the pain that darkened her eyes at that 'once in a lifetime'.

'Certainly, that's how it was with Roberto and my mother. He lost his heart to her when she was still married to my father. So when Papa died he was there to help her through. And Cesare has only ever wanted Megan. He waited for years for her because of a promise to her father.'

'I know. Megan told me.'

And because of that she had known just how much Gio had loved his Lucia. She had understood the lightning-strike of true passion when it had hit. Hadn't she felt something of the same when she had first set eyes on Gio in that hotel bar? She hadn't been able to take her eyes off him then and hadn't been able to put him out of her mind ever since.

'She also said that you and Lucia threatened to run away together if your parents didn't agree to the marriage.'

'The *fuitina*?'

Gio paused in his restless pacing and his mouth quirked up at one corner.

'Yes, we threatened that—both families thought we were far too young to know our own minds. They wanted us to separate—live a little—before we committed ourselves to each other. But we had no doubts.'

'What exactly is a *fuitina*?'

Terrie knew that she was just asking the question to keep the conversation going and because she didn't know what else to say. She had to take a couple of much-needed seconds to pull herself together, adjust to the bruises on her heart where Gio's words had landed, unknowingly wounding her, and the unfamiliar Sicilian term seemed the best possible distraction she could find.

'It's from Sicilian history—but sometimes it still happens today. Basically it just means running away together and it was used as a declaration of how serious your feelings were. It was a way for young lovers to be able to sleep together without moral condemnation.'

'And would you have done it?'

She didn't need the answer. It was there in his face; in his eyes. He would have done that and more if it had been the only way to win his Lucia.

'We both would. But in the end we didn't have to do anything quite so drastic. Our parents agreed to our engagement if I promised to concentrate hard on my studies, work at my training to be a lawyer. We were nineteen when we married.'

'So young.'

'Yeah—but we just couldn't wait any longer…crazy, weren't we?'

'But perhaps you guessed, perhaps you sensed that it wasn't going to be—that you weren't going to be together forever. Perhaps you wanted to grab at what you had while you had it.'

She'd hit a vulnerable point there, Terrie thought, watching his eyes cloud. Wanting to erase the distress, she rushed on.

'Tell me about her—what was she like?'

Did she really want to know this? she wondered as soon as she asked the question. But, strangely, as Gio started to speak she found that, contrary to what she had expected, his memories didn't hurt. Instead she found they intrigued and absorbed her, telling her so much more about the man himself as he told her about the woman he had loved and lost.

She learned what he had been like as an adolescent and a young man. How hard he had worked to become the lawyer his mother wanted him to be—and to be able to support his new young wife in spite of the fact that his family was rich in its own right. She discovered the interests they had shared together, the simple joys that meant so much more than huge, great gestures. The personal, intimate things between a man and his wife.

But she also found out the deepest, most important things about Gio himself. She learned how he loved, why he loved. She learned how he felt about honesty and faithfulness; how he had handled the arguments, the problems and the disappointments that came the way of every marriage. He told her of his joy when he had learned that Lucia was pregnant, the magical moment when his son was born. He told her of his dreams of a large family, dreams that were tragically never to come true.

And she learned how he had suffered and grieved when Lucia had been snatched away from him far, far too soon. He didn't trouble to hide the tears then; clearly felt no shame at the way they filled his eyes, dampened his cheeks and left the lush black lashes clumped together in thick, dark spikes. And Terrie respected him for that. And her heart twisted in sorrow, for both Gio and poor, pretty Lucia, who had not had long enough to share their love together.

She didn't know how long she sat there in the stillness of the night, listening to the words pouring from him. Didn't know whether hours or even days had passed, or simply minutes as she was held absorbed. She only knew that she wouldn't have wanted to lose a single second of them, even though they brought to her the most devastating personal realisation that she had ever known. One that would never leave her, and which could do nothing but change her life once and forever.

Because by the time Gio had finished his tale of love, she recognised just what had happened to her.

She had fallen in love with this man, as hopelessly, desperately and totally as he had been in love with his wife. And, like Gio, hers was a once-in-a-lifetime kind of love. One she would never feel for anyone else.

But Gio had loved and lost another woman. And, as a result, she could never have the true strength of all that his heart was capable of.

'Can I ask you something?' she said at last, when he had stopped speaking, stopped pacing, and was simply standing, one hand resting on the worktop of a cabinet, just within reach of her own.

He looked exhausted, shadows darkening the olive skin of his face, deep lines scored from his nose to his mouth. But the ebony eyes were clear and calm. It was as if he had been through a storm, a violent whirlwind, and come out the other side.

'Anything,' Gio said huskily, rawly.

And strangely enough he sounded as though he meant it.

'That night…'

She knew she didn't have to say which one. That there was only one night she could mean. The night they had met.

'You said once that Lucia died ten days before Paolo's birthday. Was—that night…?'

'That night was the second anniversary of the date she died, yes.'

'Oh, Gio…'

She reached out, touched his hand. And knew from his total stillness how much it meant.

His dark gaze went to where her fingers rested lightly over the top of his and lingered for a moment. Then he looked up again, ebony eyes locking with blue-grey. And holding.

Terrie would never know which one of them moved first. Or whether in fact they both acted in the space of the same heartbeat, heading towards each other on the impulse of almost the same thought.

She was only aware of being on her feet, and needing to be close to him. And finding that was easier than she had ever anticipated because he had halved the short distance between them too. So that all that it needed was a couple of swift, short steps and she was there, with him, his arms closing round her, her face lifting for his kiss.

It was a kiss that seemed to draw her soul out from her body, taking with it every thought of hesitation, of reservation, of second thoughts. She had no time for doubts, no time for anything but the deep-felt need to hold this man, to touch him, kiss him, give him everything that was there in her heart for him.

But most of all to give him herself.

There was a faint, inexplicable awkwardness about the way that Gio was holding her. An unsettled, uncomfortable feeling across her shoulders and back so that she wriggled slightly, trying to adjust, coming briefly out of the haze of need as she heard Gio's faint laughter that warmed her skin with his breath.

'What…?' she asked and looked up, puzzled, into his smiling eyes.

'Hands off,' Gio whispered, his smile a wide, wicked grin. 'You gave me my orders—while we're in Sicily it's strictly—'

'Oh, to hell with hands off!' Terrie exclaimed, but then suddenly she changed her mind. 'On second thoughts…'

His uncertain, slightly wary glance was all that it took to have her mouth curling in teasing mischief as she snuggled closer, rubbing her face against his chin where the rough suggestion of his growth of beard snagged against her delicate skin.

'Perhaps we'll stick to hands off,' she murmured, deliberately pitching her voice as a husky purr. 'But just for you—for me it's definitely hands *on*. I get to touch all I want!'

Slowly, tantalisingly she walked her fingers up the front of his shirt, feeling his quick catch of breath in the first second that she touched. For a moment she lingered, tracing teasing circles around the knot of his tie, round and round, until she saw him swallow, moistening the dryness of his lips.

With another cat-that-got-the-cream smile, she tugged the knot slightly loose. Paused. Tugged again.

'Teresa…'

With a low chuckle deep in her throat, she laid a reproving finger over his mouth, silencing him as she shook her head.

'My turn,' she whispered. 'Mine.'

She drew out the removal of the tie for as long as she dared, fixing her entire concentration on easing the elegant knot open, sliding the burgundy silk free. And it was only when at last it hung loose around his neck that she realised how completely still Gio had become, frozen, hardly breathing, it seemed, all his attention fixed on her.

'Good…'

She caught hold of both ends of the tie, tugged again, drawing his head forward until all she had to do was to reach up and press a long, lingering kiss on his waiting lips. His sigh of response widened the smile on her own mouth.

'You see,' she told him softly. 'Patience is rewarded—in the end.'

It was an effort to ease away from the kiss, decidedly harder to ignore the heated, tingling sensations sparking off all over her body. But she had started on a plan of how to play this and she wanted to carry it through.

The slow, careful unbuttoning of his shirt was accompanied by the heavy, pounding thud of Gio's heart just underneath her fingertips whenever they rested on the heated satin of his skin. Occasionally she paused to trace delicate erotic patterns over the lines of his chest, tangling gently in the dark hair, moving along the curves of his ribcage. When she circled first one and then the second of the dark, tight male nipples with infinite care Gio could not hold back a groan of yearning response.

'Teresa…' he muttered and his voice was thicker, hoarser than before. 'Let me…'

'No.' Her tone was firm. 'Hands off…'

But then, looking into the black pools of his eyes, she weakened, just a little.

'All right,' she conceded. 'You can kiss me…'

It was a kiss that almost broke her resolve, because, forbidden to use his hands, he let his mouth tell her how hungry and aroused he was. How much he wanted her. His hard body strained against hers, awakening the same demanding craving in her own flesh, making her wish that he would just ignore her instructions, her command, and grab for her, haul her into his arms, swing her off the floor and then carry her upstairs to his bed.

But then she risked another glance up into his face, seeing the glaze of desire settle on those brilliant eyes, the tautening of every muscle in the set of burning passion. And she knew that if her resolve to hold to this game she had started was weakening then his had hardened, become immovable. There was no backing out now. And as if to confirm her suspicions, almost, she felt, to indicate that he could read her mind, he smiled straight into her considering eyes.

'Next move, *carina*,' he challenged softly. 'I'm in your hands. But don't you think that, if we're to take this game to its natural conclusion, we might be a little more comfortable in the bedroom?'

But the bedroom was not what Terrie had in mind. The bedroom was the one he had used during his marriage. The one he had shared with Lucia. And so she caught hold of the two sides of his shirt, now gaping wildly over his bronzed chest, and led him by them out of the kitchen and across the hall, into the spacious lounge. Once there, she eased the loosened garment from him, tracing the path of the material as it slid away with her mouth, pressing kisses against his heated skin.

With her hands on the narrow leather belt at his waist, for the first time she lost a little of her confidence, hesitated slightly, but Gio sensed her feelings and shook his head in teasing reproach.

'You can't stop now, *belleza*,' he told her, and the forceful jut of his erection just below her hands gave an added emphasis to the growing urgency in his voice.

An urgency that now infected Terrie as, with rather more haste and rather less finesse, she dealt with the belt, slid off what remained of his clothing and cast them aside onto the nearest chair.

Only then, when he was naked and proudly erect before her, did she turn her attention to her own clothes. The dress was easily pulled up and over her head, the small slivers of silk that were her underwear soon followed, and as she turned back to Gio she heard the harsh, rough-edged breath that hissed in through his clenched teeth. The sound of a man very close to the edge of his control.

'*Teresa!*' he said and it was a groan of desperation. 'Have mercy on me...'

And because it was what she wanted too she nodded slowly, her smile wide and triumphant.

'*Now,*' she said. 'Now you can touch.'

And from the first moment that his hands made contact with her body she was lost, caught up in a whirlwind of sensation such as she had never known before. His fingers woke, teased, tormented, tantalised until she was a screaming mass of awareness and hunger, the need of him like a white-hot pulse at the very core of her being.

With his mouth still on her breast, Gio intuitively fulfilled her fantasy of just moments before, lifting her from her feet and tumbling her down onto the huge, soft cushions of the settee, coming after her in a hungry rush. His long legs nudged hers apart, the heated force of his masculinity straining at the juncture of her thighs, his hands sliding under her buttocks, lifting her up, tilting her so that she was perfectly ready for him.

'Now I can touch,' he muttered, more raw and rougher

than ever before. 'Now I can touch—and now I can do *this*...'

The last word was a sound of triumph and the deepest satisfaction all in one as he thrust his hotly aroused body deep into hers, taking, filling, making her his once and for all.

It was only seconds from that moment, only the space of a few, heated, throbbing heartbeats before Terrie felt all trace of control slipping from her, her body curving, arching against his, her senses climbing, peaking, shattering and taking her with him over the edge and into the oblivion of ecstasy.

She had no idea when she surfaced again, how long it had been, what had woken her. But she slowly opened her eyes to find that Gio was awake, his head propped up on one hand, dark eyes watching her with a disturbing intensity.

'Hi!' she murmured, smiling, and felt a twist of apprehension when the smile was not returned but was met with a long, thoughtful stare. 'What...?'

'I've been thinking,' he said slowly. 'About this agreement of ours. How would you feel if I said that I don't want you to go? I want you to stay here?'

'Gio...' Terrie could hardly believe what she was hearing. 'Are you saying that you...?'

She broke off, the swift rush of joy subsiding just as fast as it had come as he closed his eyes, shutting himself off from her.

'Don't, Teresa,' he said with difficulty. 'Don't ask me to give you anything more than I can manage. I'll give you what I can... You mustn't ask for more.'

His eyes opened again, burning straight into her uncertain grey ones.

'All I can...'

And would that be enough? Terrie was forced to ask herself. Feeling as she did about him, could she cope with that?

But then Gio reached for her, his arms closing round her. He kissed her, his hands smoothing down the length of her body, stirring and awakening the heady clamour that drowned out the ability to think straight—to think at all.

And it all began again.

CHAPTER TWELVE

TERRIE walked back into the bedroom slowly and reluctantly, her heart twisting on a painful combination of relief and distress when she realised that the room was empty. Gio had gone downstairs and she was alone. If she listened hard she could hear the sounds of him moving about in the kitchen.

And she could only pray that for the moment at least he would stay there. That he would give her some time to be on her own and think.

Time to adjust to what she had just discovered.

She wasn't pregnant.

She had known it as soon as she had woken up that morning. The familiar aching feeling low down in her body had told its own story. But still she had hoped.

Until now.

Now she knew for certain. Wild and rash as her behaviour with Gio had been on that first night, it had not had any permanent consequences. She was not carrying Gio's baby.

'How would you feel if I said that I don't want you to go? I want you to stay here?'

Gio's words, whispered to her in the dark of the night, came back to haunt her, whirling round and round in her head, impossible to get a grip on.

How had he meant them? Had he really meant them at all?

She knew she didn't dare to put any great reliance on anything that had been said in the heated intensity of the night they had just shared. Adrift on a sea of emotion and passion, she suspected that Gio could have said *anything*, his grip on his tongue lost completely.

But would he still keep to what he had said in the cold light of day?

Especially when he discovered that there was no baby. That the whole reason for her being here at all did not exist.

He would never have asked her to come to Sicily if he hadn't feared she might be pregnant. And she had seen enough of him with Paolo to understand why. He was a wonderful father, loving, devoted, caring. And he would have been the same with any child they had created between them.

But did he care enough about *her* to want her without that child?

'Teresa!'

Gio was calling to her, his voice coming up the stairs from the hallway below.

'Are you coming down? I made coffee—*again*.'

The joke snagged on a raw spot on Terrie's nerves, tugging painfully. She didn't need any reminder of the fact that, once again, they had left their coffee made and poured but growing cold in the mugs as they lost themselves in the inferno of passion that had reached out to swallow them up. She knew already, better than anyone, just how her desire for Gio, the hunger that he could awaken with just a touch, a kiss, a look, could sweep anything and everything else from her mind and leave her incapable of any rational thought.

And it had the same effect on Gio.

So there was no way she could trust the words he had whispered to her. Not until he repeated them to her in totally different circumstances. And when she had told him her news about the baby.

'Teresa!'

'Yes! I'm coming!'

She was already dressed in a pale blue sundress, her hair freshly washed and drying naturally in the warmth of the morning, so she had no excuse to prevaricate any longer. And the note of impatience in Gio's voice told her that if she didn't go down to him then he would come up here to find her.

Gio felt a rush of relief when he finally heard Terrie's footsteps on the stairs and knew she was on her way down at last. She had spent so long delaying upstairs that he had begun to wonder if something was wrong. If there was some reason that she didn't want to face him.

While he couldn't wait to see her. Last night had been a major turning point for him. He hadn't slept so well in a very long time—two years, in fact—and he had woken clear-headed and alert, ready to look at the future in a whole new light.

'Come on, it's getting cold!'

The ring of the doorbell sounded through his shout and with a muttered curse he dumped his own coffee mug down on the table and went to answer it.

Terrie was just reaching the bottom step as he passed in the hall.

'Hi!'

His greeting, like his wave, was swift and offhand. All he was interested in was getting to the door, dealing with whoever was there, and sending them on their way again. He wanted no interruptions, no one else intruding on his plans for Teresa and today.

'Breakfast's in the kitchen. I'll be with you in a minute.'

As he opened the door the sun streamed into the hall, blinding him for a moment, so that he had to blink hard before he could make out the small, stout black-haired woman who stood outside. But when he did, his heart sank.

'Rosa...*buon giorno*...'

Of all the times for Lucia's mother to decide to pay one of her infrequent visits, this had to be the worst she could choose. They had never got on well together, even when her daughter had been alive, and since Lucia's death their relationship had been strained at best, even though he tried to ensure that she saw plenty of Paolo, her grandson. But she only called at the house on very rare occasions. And he knew why she was here this time.

The coming Sunday was the anniversary of Lucia's birthday. And Rosa was here to arrange the trip to the cemetery to leave flowers as they had done each year.

'I...' he began but Rosa clearly wasn't listening. Instead she was staring past him, over his shoulder, her eyes fixed in an expression of disbelief.

'Who...?' she demanded in furious Italian. 'Who is *that*!'

Gio didn't have to turn to look to know who she meant. Clearly Terrie had paused at the bottom of the stairs, not making her way into the kitchen as he had suggested. He groaned inwardly. There never would be a good way for Rosa to meet the new woman in his life. But this was definitely not the best.

Inevitably, it had hit the older woman desperately hard when her daughter had died. Something of her had died with Lucia, and she had never recovered.

Half turning, he glanced to where Terrie stood behind him. She looked pale, he noted in concern. If only Rosa hadn't appeared, then he could find out what was wrong.

'This is Teresa,' he responded, in the same language that his mother-in-law had used, hoping that that would be enough.

It wasn't.

'And *who* is Teresa?' Rosa asked, bristling with antagonism. 'What is she doing here?'

He could answer that very simply and quickly—if only it was *Teresa* he was talking to. But it was Rosa who had asked the question. Rosa, who he knew would never leave until she had had an answer.

And Rosa had no right to be the first to know how he truly felt about Terrie. Certainly not before he had told Terrie herself.

But he had to say something. Anything. Something that would convince Rosa.

It was then that he remembered a conversation he had had with his mother-in-law a couple of months ago, just before he had set off on his trip to England. He snatched at the memory on a rush of relief as he turned back to Rosa.

'She's the person we talked about, remember?'

He kept to Italian, knowing Terrie spoke very little of the language.

'When we discussed getting a nanny for Paolo. An English nanny—someone who could look after him in his own home when I had to be away.'

To his relief he saw a wave of comprehension cross the older woman's face and she nodded almost approvingly.

'Ah, yes, the English governess. A good idea...'

Behind him, Gio heard the faint sound of movement and relaxed slightly. Terrie was obviously heading into the kitchen; he could join her there as soon as possible and they could start the day over again.

Luckily, Rosa didn't want to linger, and it was only

another few minutes before she said her goodbyes and drove away. Shutting the door on a sigh of relief, Gio hurried to the kitchen, a wide smile on his face.

A smile that faltered, died, when he found that the room was empty. Terrie was nowhere to be seen—so where…?

A sound from up above, the creak of floorboards from someone moving about, had him striding swiftly to the stairs.

'Teresa?'

The first tug of real anxiety hit when she didn't respond to his call.

'Teresa!'

Still no response. The tug became a sharply painful twist, some sudden instinct clutching at his guts as he started to climb the stairs, steadily at first, then increasing his pace, taking them two steps at a time as he felt his panic grow.

'*Teresa!* What…?'

The first thing he saw when he pushed open the bedroom door was her case lying open on the bed.

Open and half-filled.

No!

Anxiety became the brutal clutch of fear; the terrible suspicion that everything he had dreamed of during the night, and woken up to wanting today, had all been based on nothing but just that. A dream of wanting. With no foundation in fact.

And fear made him desperate to hide the truth until he knew just what the facts were.

'What's going on here?'

The protective fury in his voice brought Terrie whirling round from where she had been standing beside the open wardrobe. The bundle of coat-hangers and dresses in her hands told their own story, but Gio couldn't believe his eyes. He didn't *want* to believe his eyes.

'What the hell do you think you're doing?'

'I should have thought that it would be obvious just what's going on!' Terrie flung at him, her voice high and tight with hostility. 'And as for what I think I'm doing— I think I'm packing and leaving. What do *you* think?'

'I think that you're damn well not going anywhere. Not without some sort of explanation. Some reason why...'

'A reason?' Terrie echoed cynically. 'You want a reason?'

'I think you owe me one.'

'I owe you nothing. Nothing at all. So you needn't think you can order me around—demanding this and demanding that. I've nothing to give you. I came here and stayed with you because you insisted on it. And now I'm leaving—end of story.'

'No.'

Gio could only shake his head in rejection and confusion. He could almost believe that in the middle of the night, while he had been deep in the sleep of exhaustion created by the after-effects of their passionate lovemaking, someone had crept into the house and taken away the Teresa he knew. Leaving behind a clone of her, someone who was identical in looks, but totally different in personality.

'No. I'm not having that. You know why you're here! You know what our agreement was. That you would stay for four weeks—'

'Or until we were sure that I wasn't pregnant,' Terrie inserted coldly. 'I believe that was what we agreed on.'

'Teresa, what the hell are you talking about? Just what do you mean?'

'Exactly what I said...'

Terrie's hands tightened on the clothes she held, crushing the material convulsively.

'You invited me here to make sure that there was no—repercussion from our night together in the hotel. Well, you can rest assured of that.'

She tossed the dresses down, heedless of the way they fell roughly into the case. The grey eyes blazed like burning stars, brilliant in her pale face. And it was only now that he saw how her cheeks were streaked with the barely dried traces of tears.

'I'm not pregnant,' she declared starkly.

Gio's English totally deserted him.

'*Come?*' he said. '*Come te dice?* Teresa...'

What was happening? How had they come from the glorious, wonderful night they had shared to *this*? And why had she been weeping? If she was as determined to leave him as she seemed, then what in hell had upset her?

'Do you want me to say it again?'

Did she have to repeat it? Terrie thought miserably, blinking back the bitter tears that threatened. Wasn't it bad enough that it was true? She knew that she should be feeling some relief, a sense of gratitude that, now that she knew what his true opinion of her was, at least she wasn't carrying his baby too. At least she could get out, without that cruel reminder of their brief affair.

But the truth was that relief was the opposite of what she felt. That inside she was dying of loss and desolation. And if she could have done she would have welcomed any reminder of the man she loved so desperately. But she had been denied even that.

'My period started this morning. There—is that blunt enough for you? I'm not pregnant with your child, so you have no obligation to me. You don't need to look after me or support me—or—or anything. Four weeks, we said—and if at the end of that time I wasn't pregnant then I could go on my way and there'd be no f-further complications.'

For a terrible second the tears welled up again, almost defeating her. But she swallowed them down fiercely, forcing herself on.

'But in the end you didn't have to wait the full four weeks—isn't that lucky? I'm not pregnant, so you don't have to waste any more time on me. I'm leaving.'

'No!'

'*Yes.*'

She couldn't face him any more so she swung back to the wardrobe, grabbing another handful of dresses. But when she turned to deposit them in her case it was to find that Gio was beside her, reaching for the clothes and wrenching them from her hands.

'I said no. You're not leaving,' he roared, stuffing them back into the cupboard and slamming the door on it. 'At least not like this. What do you think last night was all about?'

'Do you have to ask? If you don't know, then your English mustn't be quite as good as you thought. There's a nice simple word that explains last night perfectly—a nice, simple four-letter word! It's *lust*, Gio—or sex—nothing more, nothing less...'

'No! It was more than that. Much more!'

'Oh, *please*! Don't lie to me! You don't have to pretend! We're both adults.'

'I'm not lying! And I'm not pretending about anything. I don't want you to go. I want you to stay!'

'As what?'

Bitterness overwhelmed her so that she had to force the words out past the hard, tight knot in her throat.

'As a governess for Paolo? Is that it? Is that what you want?'

She saw his face change, saw realisation dawn in the depths of his eyes, and knew that at last the truth had hit home.

'You heard?'

'Of course I heard. And I understood—well, some of it. I may not know very much Italian, so I have to admit that I was a bit fazed by—what was it—*bambin*—something.'

'*Bambinaia,*' Gio supplied, his tone as flat as his expression.

'But I'd have to be pretty thick not to make a guess at *governante*, wouldn't I, Gio? I think even someone with as little Italian as me could have a go at that one. It does mean governess, doesn't it? And I presume that the first one means nanny or something—a nanny for Paolo. An *English* nanny—that's what you were looking for, isn't it?'

She was relieved to see that at least Gio had the grace not to deny it. That he nodded in silent agreement.

'An English nanny for your son—and I fell into your lap at just the right moment. An English nanny for Paolo—an English bedmate for you—and if you were truly, truly lucky, an English mother for your next baby. What was the whole plan, Gio? Did you reckon on marrying me so that I'd do it all for free? So that you didn't even have to find a nanny's wages?'

'No.'

The blazing glare he turned on her would have quelled anyone else. But Terrie was beyond feeling any more pain. Impervious to his anger as a result of her own bitter fury.

'No,' she repeated, injecting every ounce of bite she

could into the words. 'No, of course not. Because you see, *caro mio* Gio, your plan failed. I'm not going to be used as just a nanny for Paolo. And I'm not going to be just a bedmate for you. And, as I've already said, I'm—'

'You're not leaving.'

'Oh, but I am...'

She tried to reach for the wardrobe door to open it again, but Gio moved too quickly for her, ramming his foot hard up against it so that it was impossible to move.

'No you're not! I won't let you! I won't let this happen!'

'You can't stop me!'

'I'll try everything I can. And I warn you I can play dirty if I have to...'

Oh, why wouldn't he give in? Terrie was weakening, reaching the end of her emotional strength. She didn't know how much longer she could keep up this fight.

'Gio—*please*! Don't do this to me! You can't force me to stay. I'm begging you to let me go!'

The change in his face was shocking. All the anger, the furious resistance leeched from it in a rush, leaving him looking dreadfully pale and drained.

'All right,' he said slowly. 'If that's what you want.'

It was the exact opposite of what she wanted but, with the situation as it was, there was nothing else she could do. She couldn't stay here, loving him, and knowing that he had only ever wanted to use her all the time. 'Don't ask me to give you anything more than I can manage,' he had said last night, and now she knew why. He had nothing to give her, emotionally. Nothing at all.

'But I hope you're prepared.'

Terrie had been picking up the dresses he had tossed on the bed, planning on folding them, putting them in her case, but his words froze her hands. Turning, she looked at him frowningly, bruised eyes puzzled and unsure.

'Prepared for what?'

'For the fact that I will be phoning you every single night, without fail.'

'Phoning? But Gio—*why*?'

Gio rubbed the back of his hand across his eyes in a gesture that spoke strangely of exhaustion and defeat.

'Do you remember when I told you about Lucia—how I said that since she died I've never gone to sleep...?'

'Without wishing that you could tell her how much you loved her, just one more time,' Terrie supplied, wonderingly, when his voice cracked embarrassingly, preventing him from finishing the sentence. 'Yes. But I don't see what—'

'I'm *not* going to let it happen again,' Gio told her, his eyes burning into hers, his voice ringing with a harsh desperation. 'I'm not going to let another woman go out of my life and not say how I feel. If you go—if you insist on leaving, Teresa, *amata mia*—then I will do the only thing that I can. Even if you are thousands of miles away, I will have to speak to you. Have to tell you that I love you every night before I can sleep.'

'What?'

The dresses dropped from Terrie's hands and she sank down onto the bed, her legs suddenly unable to support her any more.

'You have to tell me that...'

'That I love you.'

It was low and deep and huskily sincere.

'Is that the truth?' Even though he had said it to her face, she still found it impossible to believe.

'Why else would I say it, *cara mia*?'

'Well—but you said to—to that woman...'

'To Rosa? Lucia's mother? Teresa, *carina*, you have to ignore anything I said to her. Do you truly think that I would tell her that I loved you before I even told you myself?'

'And it's *true*? I thought you would never love anyone the way you loved Lucia.'

'And I thought so too.'

Gio crouched down in front of her, taking both her hands in his, folding his strong fingers tightly over them.

'I thought that with Lucia I'd had my quota of happiness in my lifetime. After all, some people don't even get the ten years we had together. I never thought I'd be lucky enough to have it happen again.'

Lifting her hands to his mouth, he pressed a long, lingering kiss on them, and all the while his eyes locked with hers, never wavering, never hesitating for a second.

'And I thought that, because I'd loved once, if it ever did happen again it would be in exactly the same way as it had been with Lucia. I fell in love with her through liking her, and knowing that I wanted to be with her. With you it was—different.'

'How different?' The words came out jerkily, made uneven by the fast, heavy pounding of her heart.

Gio's smile was wry, slightly self-mocking.

'You knocked me off balance right from the start. I wanted you so badly, I was blind, deaf and dumb to anything else. And at first I felt guilty. I felt as if I'd betrayed Lucia by wanting another woman—as if I'd somehow been unfaithful to her.'

'I'm sure Lucia wouldn't mind. I know she'd want you to be happy.'

Gio nodded his proud, dark head slowly in agreement.

'And now I see that you're right. But I had to come to that in my own time. That's what last night was all about.

Being here, with you, being able talk about her, to share Lucia with you, it helped me to come to terms with my loss at long last. And it helped me to say goodbye to her and be ready to move on to the next stage of my life—with you…if you'll have me.'

'If I'll… Oh, Gio!'

Reaching forward, Terrie laced her hands in the jet silk of his hair, drawing his face towards her for her kiss. His mouth was so tender, so responsive, so giving that she felt tears burn at her eyes once more. But this time they were tears of the purest joy.

'But you didn't say. Even last night…'

'Even last night I was still too much of a coward. Even when I knew how much I wanted this, wanted you in my life, I didn't dare say.'

Gio sighed deeply, lifted a hand to touch her cheek with infinite gentleness.

'My own son is braver than I am. He had no hesitation in telling you that he loved you, while I did everything I could to avoid it.'

Terrie's smile of forgiveness was gentle, filled with understanding.

'He's only a child. He doesn't really understand the pain that love can bring.'

For a moment the shadows of the past clouded Gio's eyes, so that it hurt her to see them.

'I was afraid of that too,' he admitted. 'I'd lost my love once; I was terrified that it would happen again. Then I realised that by being too much of a coward to commit, I was actually creating the situation I was so afraid of. I was driving you to the point where if I didn't say what I felt then you would leave me, and I'd be back in exactly the hell I dreaded most.'

'But you'll never lose me now.'

'Are you sure?'

The intensity in his voice hit home straight to Terrie's heart like an arrow thudding into the gold.

'Are you really sure? Is that what you're saying? Because, *amata*, you...'

He broke off as realisation of what he was saying finally dawned on her, her eyes widening in shock.

'I haven't said it, have I? Oh, Gio—forgive me. Of course that's what I'm saying! I love you. I adore you. I want to spend my life with you.'

'And I you, my darling. I want to make love to you each and every night. To fall asleep in your arms, wake up and find you next to me every morning. And I promise you that each and every day of my life I will tell you how much I love you so that you need never, ever doubt it again.'

'And I'll tell you,' Terrie whispered, her mouth against his for the kiss she so desperately needed.

'We'll tell each other,' Gio vowed, and he took her lips with his to seal his promise for a lifetime.

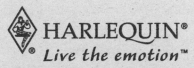

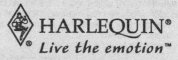

Coming Next Month

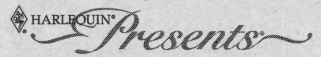

THE BEST HAS JUST GOTTEN BETTER!

#2397 THE SPANIARD'S BABY BARGAIN Helen Bianchin
Billionaire Manolo de Guardo has been dumped—by his nanny!
He needs someone to care for his daughter…fast! Ariane Celeste
is a Sydney reporter sent to interview him, and she's persuaded
to help out temporarily. But Manolo knows a good deal—and he
wants to keep Ariane….

#2398 THE PASSION PRICE Miranda Lee
When they were young Jake Winters walked out on Angelina, leaving her heartbroken and pregnant—and now he's back. Angelina is
amazed to see his transformation from bad boy
to sexy Sydney lawyer—and Jake is insistent that he will bed
Angelina one more time….

#2399 A SPANISH MARRIAGE Diana Hamilton
Javier married Zoe purely to protect her from male predators
who were tempted by her money and her beauty—he has all the
money he could ever need. But as their paper marriage continues
he finds it increasingly hard to resist his wife—even though he
made her a promise….

#2400 THE FORBIDDEN BRIDE Sara Craven
Zoe Lambert inherits a Greek island villa and sets off for a
new start in life. Her new home is perfect—and so is the sexy gardener who comes with it! But when Zoe discovers that Andreas
isn't just a gardener, but the wealthy son of a shipping tycoon, several startling events occur….

#2401 THE TYCOON'S VIRGIN BRIDE Sandra Field
One night Jenessa's secret infatuation with tycoon
Bryce Laribee turned to passion—but the moment he
discovered she was a virgin he walked out! Twelve years
later, the attraction between them is just as mind-blowing,
and Bryce is determined to finish what they started.

#2402 MISTRESS BY AGREEMENT Helen Brooks
From the moment tycoon Kingsley Ward walks into her office
Rosie recognizes the sexual invitation in his eyes. Kingsley's initial
purpose had been business, not pleasure. But Rosie is beautiful
and—unbelievably!—seems immune to his charms. Kingsley
decides he will pursue her….